You're Always a

Privileged

Woman.

INTRODUCING
PAGES & PRIVILEGES™.

It's our way of thanking you for buying
our books at your favorite retail store.

GET ALL THIS FREE
WITH JUST ONE PROOF OF PURCHASE:

◆ **Hotel Discounts** up
to 60% at home and
abroad ◆ **Travel Service**
- Guaranteed lowest
published airfares
plus 5% cash back

$50 VALUE

on tickets ◆ **$25 Travel Voucher**

◆ **Sensuous Petite Parfumerie** collection

◆ **Insider Tips Letter**
with sneak previews
of upcoming books

*You'll get a FREE personal card, too.
It's your passport to all these benefits– and to
even more great gifts & benefits to come!*

There's no club to join. No purchase commitment. No obligation.

Enrollment Form

☐ *Yes!* I WANT TO BE A *Privileged Woman.*

Enclosed is one *PAGES & PRIVILEGES*™ Proof of Purchase from any Harlequin or Silhouette book currently for sale in stores (Proofs of Purchase are found on the back pages of books) and the store cash register receipt. Please enroll me in *PAGES & PRIVILEGES*™. Send my Welcome Kit and FREE Gifts -- and activate my FREE benefits -- immediately.

More great gifts and benefits to come like these luxurious Truly Lace and L'Effleur gift baskets.

NAME (please print)

ADDRESS   APT. NO

CITY   STATE   ZIP/POSTAL CODE

PROOF OF PURCHASE ~~SAMPLE OF ONLY~~

NO CLUB!
NO COMMITMENT!
Just one purchase brings you great Free Gifts and Benefits!
(More details in back of this book.)

Please allow 6-8 weeks for delivery. Quantities are limited. We reserve the right to substitute items. Enroll before October 31, 1995 and receive one full year of benefits.

Name of store where this book was purchased_____

Date of purchase_____

Type of store:

☐ Bookstore   ☐ Supermarket   ☐ Drugstore

☐ Dept. or discount store (e.g. K-Mart or Walmart)

☐ Other (specify)_____

Which Harlequin or Silhouette series do you usually read?

_____

Complete and mail with one Proof of Purchase and store receipt to:

U.S.: *PAGES & PRIVILEGES*™, P.O. Box 1960, Danbury, CT 06813-1960

Canada: *PAGES & PRIVILEGES*™, 49-6A The Donway West, P.O. 813, North York, ON M3C 2E8   **PRINTED IN U.S.A**

Marriage. To Matt Taylor.

Dani looked into his eyes. What did she see there? Affection? Yearning? Horror? She couldn't tell. Her heart skipped. She gulped down her own mixed dose of fear and excitement. Was this the lesser of two evils or the best of both worlds?

She swallowed hard and tipped her chin up. "I think Matt and I would make excellent partners—um, parents—Judge Haroucourt. I mean…" She glanced at Matt for help.

"She means, she's willing to give me the answer to the question I intended to ask in that restaurant months ago." He took her hands. His eyes sparkled but his smile seemed tinged with sadness as he finished his statement. "Danielle McAdams has agreed to be my wife."

Dear Reader,

Ah, summertime...those lazy afternoons and sultry nights. The perfect time to find romance with a mysterious stranger in a far-off land, or right in your own backyard—with an irresistible Silhouette Romance hero. Like Nathan Murphy, this month's FABULOUS FATHER. Nathan had no interest in becoming a family man, but when Faith Reynolds's son, Cory, showed him *The Daddy List*, Nathan couldn't help losing his heart to the boy, and his pretty mom.

The thrills continue as two strong-willed men show their women how to trust in love. Elizabeth August spins a stirring tale for ALWAYS A BRIDESMAID! in *The Bridal Shower*. When Mike Flint heard that Emma Wynn was about to marry another man, he was determined to know if her love for him was truly gone, or burning deep within. In Laura Anthony's *Raleigh and the Rancher* for WRANGLERS AND LACE, ranch hand Raleigh Travers tries her best to resist ranch owner Daniel McClintock. Can Daniel's love help Raleigh forget her unhappy past?

Sometimes the sweetest passions can be found right next door, or literally on your doorstep, as in Elizabeth Sites's touching story *Stranger in Her Arms* and the fun-filled *Bachelor Blues* by favorite author Carolyn Zane.

Natalie Patrick makes her writing debut with the heartwarming *Wedding Bells and Diaper Pins*. Winning custody of her infant godson seemed a lost cause for Dani McAdams until ex-fiancé Matt Taylor offered a marriage of convenience. But unexpected feelings between them soon began to complicate their convenient arrangement!

Happy Reading!

Anne Canadeo
Senior Editor

Please address questions and book requests to:
Silhouette Reader Service
U.S.: 3010 Walden Ave., P.O. Box 1325, Buffalo, NY 14269
Canadian: P.O. Box 609, Fort Erie, Ont. L2A 5X3

WEDDING BELLS AND DIAPER PINS

Natalie Patrick

Silhouette
R O M A N C E™
Published by Silhouette Books
America's Publisher of Contemporary Romance

To Beth Harbison and Stephanie Hauk for their good taste in liking my work.
And to Catherine Bernardi for supporting me and her long-distance phone company devoutly.

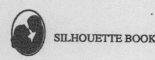 SILHOUETTE BOOKS

ISBN 0-373-19095-6

WEDDING BELLS AND DIAPER PINS

Copyright © 1995 by Luanne Jones

All rights reserved. Except for use in any review, the reproduction or utilization of this work in whole or in part in any form by any electronic, mechanical or other means, now known or hereafter invented, including xerography, photocopying and recording, or in any information storage or retrieval system, is forbidden without the written permission of the editorial office, Silhouette Books, 300 East 42nd Street, New York, NY 10017 U.S.A.

All characters in this book have no existence outside the imagination of the author and have no relation whatsoever to anyone bearing the same name or names. They are not even distantly inspired by any individual known or unknown to the author, and all incidents are pure invention.

This edition published by arrangement with Harlequin Enterprises B.V.

® and TM are trademarks of Harlequin Enterprises B.V., used under license. Trademarks indicated with ® are registered in the United States Patent and Trademark Office, the Canadian Trade Marks Office and in other countries.

Printed in U.S.A.

NATALIE PATRICK

believes in romance and has had firsthand experience to back up that belief. She met her husband in January and married him in April of that same year—they would have eloped sooner but friends persuaded them to have a real wedding. Ten years and two children later she knows she's found her real romantic hero.

Amid the clutter in her work space, she swears that her headstone will probably read: She Left This World A Brighter Place But Not Necessarily A Cleaner One. She certainly hopes her books brighten her readers' days.

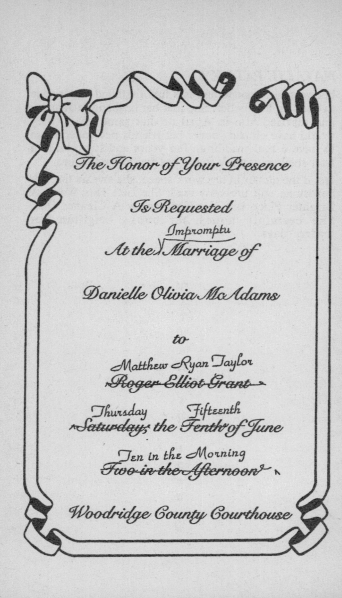

The Honor of Your Presence

Is Requested

Impromptu

At the ~~At the~~ Marriage of

Danielle Olivia McAdams

to

Matthew Ryan Taylor

~~Roger Elliot Grant~~

Thursday *Fifteenth*

~~Saturday, the Tenth of June~~

Ten in the Morning

~~Two in the Afternoon~~

Woodridge County Courthouse

Prologue

"Danielle Olivia McAdams, do you take this man to be your lawfully wedded husband, to have and to hold from this day forward, till death do you part?"

Dani felt the heat of every eye in the judge's chambers zeroing in on her. The hairs on the back of her neck pricked up. A bead of sweat trickled from her nape down the length of her rigid spine. She turned to the tall man beside her. This was it. The culmination of six months of dating and countless hours discussing the practicality of uniting two such like minds.

Love had never been an issue in those conversations with Roger Grant. He found the emotion a cumbersome bother, and she... Well, if she had ever had any delusions about romance and happily-ever-afters, Matthew Taylor had long since dispelled them. No, this was the best thing for both of them and the sooner she gave her answer, the sooner she could get on with her life.

She lifted her gaze to Roger's taut face. Through the fine tulle of her veil, she watched him stretch his mouth into a half smile, half grimace. He gave her hand a squeeze. Dani could feel the bones beneath the damp skin of his palm. She forced a smile onto her lips.

"I..." She craned her neck. Her mother's pearl necklace made a delicate rattling sound, then seemed to tighten like a tourniquet around her throat. "I..."

She pressed her lips together and bowed her head. Late-afternoon sunlight glinted off the deep brunette hair tumbling around her slender shoulders. A sickly floral scent drifted up from the loose rose bouquet she had chosen for the impromptu nuptials. The deep red petals, edged in black from a day's decay, trembled in her white-knuckled grasp.

She swallowed to push down the hard lump of cold doubt that had lodged high in her chest. Her lips parted as she tried to speak. A murmur swept through the friends and relatives hastily gathered to observe this milestone. She filled her lungs. The crowd drew a collective breath, like some great chorus preparing to launch into a prolonged reprise.

"I..." From somewhere in the crowd, a baby's wail rattled the uneasy quiet. The familiar sound pierced Dani's consciousness. She froze.

Roger tensed. He gripped her hand.

She cast her gaze downward.

He shut his eyes and released an irritated sigh.

She whispered, "I can't."

"What?" Roger pulled away from her. He clamped his hands on his angular hipbones and glowered at her. "Have you gone stark-raving mad, Dani?"

The wedding guests gasped in unison. Dani's stomach lurched and heat scalded her cheeks.

Fury flashed in Roger's usually emotionless eyes.

She seized his sleeve and dug her fingers into the expensive fabric. "Roger, please, I've had a change of heart about ne baby. It's only fair you know before we take our vows nat I plan on keeping him."

Dani heard her mother's emphatic approval above the oices of the crowd. Suddenly, she wished she could make me stand still for everyone else so she and Roger could have moment of privacy to talk this out. In lieu of that, she ettled for stepping behind a large silk floral spray rented for ne wedding. She pulled Roger's sleeve to drag him along.

He stumbled the few steps after her, then yanked his arm ut of her grasp. The congregation took this as a sign they ould speak softly among themselves. Dani hoped the vhispered speculations would screen out the hushed con-ersation between her and Roger. Drawing in her breath, she aced him with confidence. "I can't, in good conscience, and that baby over to uncaring cousins who are only tak-ng him to appease the family patriarch and secure their own nheritances."

"So, you want to burden me with him?" Roger tipped his ead down to scowl at her and his glasses fell forward, naking his eyes seem unnaturally large. "Have you forgot-en the plans we made—that you'd work double shifts at the ospital until you got pregnant and then you'd quit? You an't do that tethered down by that baby."

"Yes, but..."

"Dani, the main reason we decided to proceed with this narriage was that we were both so anxious to start our own amily."

"And what better way to start than with little Kyle?"

"A better way to start—the only way for me—is with a hild of our own." He stabbed his glasses back into place vith one long finger. "Why are you doing this, Dani? Two veeks ago, when you were saddled with that squalling brat, rou swore it wouldn't change a thing between us. Now rou're saying you want to bring the drooling rug rat into my nome. If that's not madness, what is it?"

"Love." The word was barely audible to her own ears, but Roger's expression told her he'd heard it.

"Love? How could you love him? You'd never seen as much as a photo of him until he got left with you by mistake."

"It wasn't a mistake. I'm convinced of that now. The court-appointed guardian brought him here because this is where he belongs. He *is* my godson," Dani argued. "I promised to be responsible for him if anything happened to his parents."

"You've hardly seen those people since they went to Alaska a few years ago." Roger crossed his arms over his chest.

"Nevertheless, I did make that promise. Even though I've lost contact with Bill and Karen Delaney, this baby needs someone to take care of him." She angled her chin up. Her veil fell against her lips but she continued her passionate speech. "I have the legal and moral obligation to look after the best interests of the child."

"That obligation isn't yours alone." His eyes narrowed to slits. "Why can't the child's godfather take him?"

"His godfather?" Dani staggered backward a step. Her heartbeat pounded violently in her ears as she found the courage to say, "Matt Taylor is in no position to care for an infant."

"Why not? It's not as if Taylor will raise it like he was raised, dressing it in rags or skipping out on the rent in the dead of night." Roger's gaunt face lit with superior glee.

Pain and guilt slashed Dani's heart. How dare he talk about Matt like that, she seethed in silence.

"Matt Taylor is the very definition of success." She slapped her withering bouquet against the gently belled skirt of her silk gown. Dozens of red petals rained down onto the floor. "But that success has a price. He's totally committed to his law practice. He doesn't have the patience for any re

ationship, especially not one as demanding as parent-
hood.''

"Did you ask him if he would take the child to raise?"
Roger pressed again.

For the first time since the proceedings had started, the
guests went totally silent. Dani stared up at Roger but in her
mind the face she saw belonged to Matt. Fat tears beaded up
into her line of vision and she tightened her grip on the
bouquet in her hand. Across the hushed room, the baby's
content gurgle reached her. She jerked her head up and
pointed at Roger with the disheveled flowers in her fist.
"Matt Taylor isn't the issue here. The baby is. He's my priority now and I intend to give him a home, with or without
you."

"If you keep that baby, it will be without me."

"Fine." She slammed the bouquet into his chest and spun
around in a shower of petals and greenery. In a few steps,
she had gathered up her soon-to-be-son and rushed out into
the bright June afternoon.

Chapter One

Matt Taylor cocked his wrist. He cursed, then hurled the dart in his hand with an accuracy borne of long-burning anger. The feather-trimmed projectile whistled through the air seeking its mark. With a muffled pop, the menacing brass point pierced the photograph attached to the circular board.

"Bull's-eye." Matt let out a low, cynical laugh and strode the length of his decidedly masculine den to admire his handiwork up close. A cropped ridge of feathers scraped his palm as he pulled the dart free. He squinted at the hole in the throat of his target.

Serves you right. He raised his gaze to his own face above the puncture mark. Matt had been nineteen when the photo had been taken. He and his date had attended the prom in their high school's gym. Time, he'd been told, had been exceedingly kind to him. He didn't see it. Sure, his thick brown hair hadn't receded and he still had a lean, athletic body. But when he looked in the mirror, he couldn't deny the faint

ines etched around his brown eyes. And he couldn't deny a
onging in those eyes that had not been there in his callow
youth. That hunger, for a life he had put off in favor of establishing his law practice, shone more clearly with each
passing year.

Matt sputtered out a laugh bitter with irony. All those
years striving to create the kind of financial security he had
never known as a child—and what had it cost him? Despite
his status as the most successful lawyer in his small home-
town of Woodbridge, Indiana, the thing he yearned for
most was the one thing his ne'er-do-well dad had always
had—the love of a wife and family.

Fat chance of that now. Today, the one woman he would
always love was marrying another man. He glanced down
at his wristwatch.

"Make that *has married,*" he said, correcting himself.
The hard muscles of his stomach clenched. What a jerk he'd
been for postponing their own wedding plans again and
again, until he drove her away with his single-minded am-
bition.

He scowled at the smug expression on his younger face.
Suddenly it dawned on him that when people told him he
hadn't changed since high school, they might not have
meant it as a compliment.

He gripped the icy metal of the dart between his fingers
then used the sharp point to pin the curled corner of the old
photo back in place. He planted his feet wide and made
himself focus on the figure beside him in the picture. Dani
McAdams. How beautiful she had looked in her blue prom
dress. Of course, she'd always looked beautiful to him—and
she always would.

They'd broken off their young romance not long after this
picture was taken. He'd had to work two jobs to pay his way
through college. That, on top of striving to keep his grades
up so that he could get into law school, had left no time for

a long-distance relationship. He'd never realized it before, but now it was painfully clear that putting his goals ahead of Dani then had set a terrible precedent. Yet even today he couldn't justify any other course. A career meant freedom and security. His dedication to work meant that his own children would never have to scrimp and scrape just to get a decent education.

Two years after they had posed for this photo, Dani graduated and headed to college in another state. Four years ago, she had returned to Woodbridge with her new nursing degree. And in time, they found each other again—if only temporarily. He ran one finger down the length of her image and sighed.

If only he could see Dani one more time. If only he could hear her call his name.

"Matt?"

The need was so strong in him he could almost hear her voice. He shut his eyes and the corners of his mouth tugged up in a smile that belied the pain that one tender sound inflicted.

"Can you hear me, Matt?"

His eyes flew open and focused in the direction of Dani's impatient voice. A shadow filled the curtained window of his front door. Could it be?

"Matt, if you're in there, please open the door. My hands are too full to ring the bell."

"Dani." The name blew past his parched lips. Why was she here instead of at her wedding reception? Did he dare hope she'd come to her senses and run back to him? His pulse hammered in his tight chest. Perspiration beaded on his upper lip. Dani had come back to him. Joy and anger over her sudden reappearance warred within him and for an instant, joy triumphed.

He rushed toward his front door, ready to swing it open and take the woman he loved into his arms. But as his hand closed over the knob, pride and reason chimed in.

Whoa, boy. Do you really want her to see you acting like a lovesick pup? For all you know she's brought her new husband around to make peace with you before they go off on their honeymoon.

"Matt?" The gentle imploring of her tone took on an agitated shade. "Matthew Taylor. I know you're in there. I saw your car in the driveway."

Matt steeled his backbone, but let his broad shoulders relax to give the pretense of nonchalance. He set his face in an expression of amused indifference, determined not to let Dani see his true emotions. His fingers curled around the cold doorknob.

"Matt, please, let me in. I have to see you."

Quick and neat, the way he used to make his mother rip a bandage off his skinned knees, that was how he tore open the door. "Why, hello, Dani," he said, his tone chilled by sarcasm. "Nice outfit. Is it new?"

She ought to slap him. But she needed his help too much to risk it. Dani batted her veil away from her face. She'd spent most of her life looking at Matthew Taylor through rose-colored glasses, the last thing she needed now was to see that fabulous face swathed by the romantic white mist the tulle created. "Spare me the smart remarks, Taylor. I'm in no mood to fight with you right now."

Matt crossed his well-muscled arms over his puffed-up chest. "Is that so?"

"It's so," she said through teeth so tight, the words sounded like steam escaping an old radiator. She hoisted the baby to a more secure position on her hip, then bent her knees to reach the suitcase beside her. The hard heels of her satin pumps clomped on the wooden porch. She lifted the suitcase in one hand, using it to counterbalance the squirming infant. "I'm in hot water up to my nose and you're the only one who can get me out."

If that revelation affected him, the stubborn fool wasn't going to let her see it. He simply stood back and swept his arm inward to motion her inside. She drew a deep breath of warm summer air, gripped the handle of the suitcase tighter and stepped across the threshold.

Matt let the heavy front door fall shut. Dani jumped at the sound. The suitcase slipped from her hand and clattered to the tile floor. Her gaze fluttered to the ground. She clutched the baby, then raised her eyes with confidence to Matt's face again. She couldn't swear to it, but she believed she saw a smile playing on his lips over her nervousness. In an instant it was gone and Matt's cool-eyed attention moved from her to the infant in her arms.

"Hey there, Kyle Matthew, want to come to Uncle Matt?" The baby thrust out his chubby hands and Matt took him away easily.

As the textures of Kyle's clothing skidded along Dani's palm, she resisted the urge to curl her fingers into the stretchy knit of his sweater or the nubby terry cloth of his booties. The child rested his pink cheek against Matt's hard chest and snuggled into the security of his embrace. The sight tore at Dani's battered heart. She reached out to wrap her hand around Kyle's little calf, swinging his tiny leg gently.

Matt glanced over at her, his expression annoyingly underplayed. "I thought you were supposed to turn Kyle over to his adoptive family this morning, before the wedding."

Dani gritted her teeth at the memory of the disastrous encounter with Kyle's blood relatives earlier in the day. She winced and pinched the bridge of her nose with her thumb and forefinger. "I didn't marry Roger and I didn't give up the baby." She drew a deep breath and commanded her head to stop throbbing long enough to let her get all this out. "I have no intention of doing either one. That's why I'm here."

Matt cocked his head a millimeter to the right and narrowed his eyes at her. "I don't think I follow you."

Dani fought the urge to study the toes of her shoes. This confession did not come easily to her and not knowing how it would be received made it harder still. What if Matt sneered at her? Or worse, laughed? She ran one finger inside her borrowed necklace while considering the man. Standing there with little Kyle in his arms, he looked even more appealing than ever. Surely he wouldn't let her down. Not this time. He just couldn't. Her whole future lay in his hands.

She straightened and shook her head, sending her thick curls bouncing against her back. "Like I said before, Matt, I've come here because I need your help."

Pride flickered in the depths of his brown eyes but he quickly reined it in, much to Dani's surprise. His face shone with concern and just a touch of skepticism. "You need my help as a friend, or as a lawyer?"

"Both." She met his gaze with hard determination. "As a friend, I need you to help me hide out for a few days." She tipped her head toward the suitcase she'd left lying by the door, hoping he wouldn't realize it contained her trousseau. "I'm just not ready to face the onslaught of questions and advice from friends and family about the trials of being a single mom."

Matt frowned. "It is a pretty big commitment you're taking on. Are you sure about it?"

She reached out and curved her hand over the baby's plump thigh. Kyle cooed and laid his curly blond head under Matt's chin. An indescribable love for the child welled up inside Dani. "I've never been more sure about anything in my entire life."

Matt's large hand closed over hers on the baby's leg. "Then how can I help?"

The heat of his hand enveloped her icy fingers just as the warmth of his voice permeated her chilled being. It gave her hope and the strength she needed to finish her story. "That's where your help as a lawyer comes in. I want you to represent me in the custody battle."

"Custody battle?" The words rang in Matt's ears like the sound of an open hand striking an unsuspecting cheek. "When you said you were keeping Kyle, I assumed it was with the family's consent."

"Well . . ."

If her first words were a slap in the face, her deliberate hedging was a sucker punch to the gut. "What are you telling me? That you've taken Kyle without the consent of his family?"

"Those people aren't any more his family than the man in the moon," Dani protested. "Just because they share some genetic background does not make them the best suited people to raise Kyle. For goodness' sake, Matt, they haven't even decided which of the two Delaney sisters will get 'stuck with him' as they put it."

This is how it feels to have a stroke, Matt thought, as the blood in his veins turned into a roaring torrent. He clutched the baby protectively between them. "Let me get this straight. You didn't approve of the way the baby's family talked about him, so you just kidnapped him?"

"Kidnapped?" The word crackled in the tension-filled foyer.

"Yes, kidnapped," Matt bellowed. "That's what you've done. And roped me in on your crime, to boot."

"Would you please calm down?" Dani's green eyes telegraphed a hasty warning as they moved from Matt's face to Kyle's and back again.

"Calm down?" Matt lowered his voice to a hoarse whisper, cupping his hand over the baby's exposed ear for good measure. "How can I calm down when, with this one impulsive action, you have put my career and my reputation in jeopardy?"

"I've done no such thing." She tugged the baby away from him. "The Delaneys know I have Kyle. Everything is under control. But leave it to you to boil everything down to how it affects your precious career."

"My career is about all I have left, Dani. What's wrong with wanting to protect it, and myself?"

She settled Kyle across her upper body and he immediately made use of her padded shoulder as a pillow. A tiny pool of drool darkened the elegant white fabric under his pink cheek but Dani gave it no notice. She just glowered up at Matt in silence.

For the first time, he let himself really look at her. She practically glowed in her wedding gown. The white beaded bodice accentuated the roundness of her breasts. The skirt concealed what he knew to be a fantastic pair of legs—and who knew what else. Probably some of that white lacy lingerie she'd always admired in catalogs but never could bring herself to buy until she was married. He'd once teased her for flaunting her moral superiority but even then he'd known the lingerie was symbolic of more than sexuality. All those years, Dani had put her life on hold for him. While he'd slaved away countless nights and weekends at the office, establishing his career, she'd settled for his leftover time. As a nurse, she'd lovingly cared for almost every baby born in town, yet she had no child of her own. Marriage, babies, lingerie. No wonder she'd rushed headlong into marriage with the first decent guy who'd offered real commitment.

"I'm sorry," he said, wishing it would suffice. "I didn't mean to put my concerns first. But if you had kidnapped the baby, as an officer of the court, I would have been compelled to turn you in and place Kyle where he belonged."

"He belongs with me." She folded the drowsy infant into a deep embrace.

He did belong with her. One look was all the proof Matt needed. Dani was a natural mother. Feelings he'd long suppressed rose to tangle with his words as he assured her, "I see that, and Monday morning I'll file all the necessary papers to make sure you keep him. If the Delaneys are agreeable, it shouldn't be too complicated."

Dani sank her perfect white teeth into the full center of her red lips. "Um, the Delaneys only agreed to my keeping Kyle for another week while they decided who would take him. But I have every reason to believe that they would fight tooth and nail to get custody of him."

He wasn't having a stroke. It was a heart attack. The symptoms clearly pointed to it. Heart palpitations. Cold sweats. Nausea. The inability to utter a single intelligible sentence. "Are you . . . ? Do they . . . ?"

"Shh." Dani pressed her finger to her lips and dipped her gaze to the sleeping baby. "Why don't you invite me to come in and sit down so I can tell you the whole story?"

"The den" was all he could manage to say without shouting. Or swearing.

She headed for the den, careful not to disturb the baby, then lowered herself gingerly onto the leather couch. Matt chose to lean back against his massive desk. He crossed his arms and stretched his legs out in front of him. "So, let's hear the whole long, sordid story."

"It all started this morning when the Delaney sisters, Sarah and Veronica, showed up to take Kyle. They didn't even have a car seat, that's how ill-prepared they were." She patted Kyle's back in a soothing rhythm as she rushed through the details. "Then, the whole time I was trying to go over his routine with them, telling them how he likes to be rocked at nap time, that he has to wear a sleeper to bed because he kicks off the covers and that he's just about ready to cut his first tooth…'' Her voice trailed off and her hand stilled on the child's back.

Clearly she was fighting back the tears and for an instant, Matt thought the tears would win. Then she straightened, sighed and continued with the tale.

"Anyway, all they could do was bicker about who was going to pay for the child care and accuse each other of trying to weasel out of their share of the family responsibilities."

Matt frowned. He had a very bad feeling about this.

"So, you see, it was pretty easy to persuade them to let me keep Kyle until they were ready for him." Her dark brows angled down over her stormy green eyes. "It was the first thing the two witches agreed on all morning."

"Why women like that would fight you for custody of a baby is a mystery to me."

"I can solve that mystery in one word." Dani chuckled scornfully. "Money."

He shifted. The sharp edge of the desk creased his flesh and he adjusted his position again. A few wayward papers fluttered to the ground. Matt ignored them. He narrowed his gaze on Dani and prodded her to finish. "Money? How can that be? I was Bill and Karen's lawyer. I know for a fact that their estate didn't amount to very much." It hadn't even covered the cost of the funerals. Matt had paid the balance out of his own pocket but nobody, not even Dani, knew that. "If they're taking Kyle to get his inheritance, then that's easily remedied with a quick peek at the will."

"Unfortunately it's not Kyle's inheritance they're after—it's their own."

She laid her head back and shut her eyes. He could see the exhaustion and frustration in her lovely face, but he knew she would not accept any sympathy from him about it. He could only watch and wait for her to go on with the story.

After a moment, she lifted her head. The movement set her white hat askew, the short veil clinging to her rich brunette hair. She didn't bother to adjust it. "You know when Bill married Karen, a poor girl with no family, his rich grandfather wrote him out of his will?"

Matt nodded. "According to Bill, disinheriting grandchildren is the old man's favorite pastime."

"Exactly." Dani shifted against the soft, wine-colored leather and settled more deeply into the comfortable sofa. "Now that Bill is gone, his cousins are the sole heirs to a vast fortune. They don't really want Kyle, but they can't afford to let someone else take him and risk incurring their grandfather's wrath."

"Damn." Matt swept his knuckles over his whiskered jaw, his gaze focused on the sweet, innocent child. "I had no idea."

"That's why I expect a major court battle for the baby." Dani turned her face against the soft swirls of downy blond hair on Kyle's head. She paused, took a deep breath and planted a tiny, tender kiss there. "But they say possession is nine-tenths of the law and the court-appointed guardian delivered Kyle to me, not to them. Surely that's in my favor."

He sighed and hung his head to shut out the image of Dani cuddling the baby. Thoughts, emotions and questions flew fast and furious through his mind and seeing her that way only distracted him more.

"Matt?"

"Hmm?" He pretended the carpet was the most interesting thing he'd ever seen.

"I will get to adopt Kyle, won't I?"

"Dani," he said, making himself look at her. "The sisters are blood relatives who want him. You, on the other hand, made it clear that you didn't want him—by asking the sisters to take him. That doesn't bode well for your case."

She sat up, her fingers clutching the fabric of the sleeping infant's outfit. "But I've changed my mind, Matt. I've changed my plans for the future—just to fit Kyle's needs."

"That's all well and good." He folded his arms. "But a judge might worry that you'll change your mind again and decide you don't want Kyle."

"That's not going to happen," she cried.

"You don't have to convince me." He tapped his finger to his breastbone. "I'm just telling you that the court may look at your past actions and they may be used against you."

She glanced down at the baby and sighed.

Matt hated to beleaguer the point, but it was his legal duty to stress the facts. "Dani, a judge may feel he's making the choice between placing the baby with a family who, whatever their motives, will always provide for the child or with a total stranger who has rejected him once."

"That's not true." Her voice rose. Kyle roused. They each caught their breath. The baby made a soft, suckling sound, then fell back into his deep sleep. Dani lifted her gaze to Matt, her eyes filled with desperation as she whispered, "That's not true. I never rejected Kyle and I'm not a total stranger, I'm his godmother."

"That's an honorary role, not a legal one." He was sure it hurt him as much to tell her that as it did for her to hear it.

"B-but Karen wanted me to raise him if anything happened to her." Her big green eyes flooded with tears. "I was her maid of honor when she eloped with Bill—those cousins didn't even acknowledge the marriage."

"I remember," Matt said, shaking his head.

"I'll admit," she continued in a strangled voice, "I hadn't given it much thought since we got their phone call seven months ago asking us to be Kyle's godparents. But I did accept. I was happy to." She gazed off into the distance, her face pained and pale. "The baptism was the last time I saw Karen."

"I know." He hoped the tenderness in his tone would comfort her. "I got a letter from Bill just after we'd returned, with a request to add a codicil to his will."

She swung her hopeful gaze to his face. "Then, I do have some claim on Kyle?"

He stood and focused his eyes on the empty stone fireplace at the end of the rectangular den. "If you recall, Dani, we were still together then. Bill and Karen fully expected us to marry and so we were both mentioned in the will."

"I wrote Karen about our breakup and about meeting Roger." Her voice wavered, then she sighed. "But their home was so remote, it sometimes took months for a letter to reach them."

"Right." Tension tightened his jaw so that the word came out unexpectedly hard. He straightened and walked to the hearth, attempting to give himself time to get his emotions under control. He laid his forearm over the polished wooden mantel. The stone before him gave off a chill that well suited his mood.

"But you wouldn't keep me from adopting Kyle, Matt, so there's no problem. Right?"

The upbeat lilt of the question did not fool Matt. She was near panic. He spun on his heel to meet her gaze. Treating her as he would a distraught witness, he used his steady voice and cool expression to calm her. "Bill wanted to provide for every contingency, so he asked that besides the two of us, a third party be listed as a potential guardian for Kyle."

She caressed the baby's head with her hand and bit her lip, her tear-bathed eyes riveted on Matt's face. She asked with her eyes what she could not voice.

The answer cut through the strained silence, as sure and unerring as the dart he had thrown earlier. "The third party mentioned was Bill's next of kin."

If she had been holding anything but the baby, Dani would have dropped it, leapt off the couch and shrieked. Instead she sat in silence while her world went careening crazily off kilter.

Matt placed one foot up on the grey stone of the rugged hearth, striking a casual pose. Only his balled fist on the gleaming oak mantel betrayed any anxiety. "In the strictest sense, we each have a legal claim to the baby, putting the Delaney family on equal footing to petition for custody."

She shook her head in disbelief. "Why on earth did you write that in the will? Why couldn't you have said that we would take the child and only if we didn't want him would the next of kin take him?"

Matt lifted his shoulders in something between a shrug and a cringe. "Bill wanted to cover all the bases. He was an excellent pilot but there was always risk. The fact that Karen occasionally tagged along on charter flights made him doubly concerned. This was not a mere formality in his will. He had to be sure Kyle would be cared for."

"Didn't he trust us to take Kyle?" she asked in a harsh whisper.

Matt ran his knuckles along his lightly bristled cheek. "Bill Delaney was a realist. He knew that things happened—things that no one could predict. He couldn't take the chance that we would be unavailable for Kyle."

"But you could have convinced him," she accused, choking back a sob.

"What kind of lawyer would I be if I advised my clients against their own best interests, Dani?" His jaw tightened as he answered his own rhetorical question. "A disbarred one, that's what kind."

"So, what you're saying is that once again you played the part of Matt Taylor, super lawyer. But, as usual, I somehow ended up paying for it."

He opened his mouth to respond but the shrill ringing of the telephone stopped him.

Dani's gaze riveted to the object as if it were a time bomb. It let out another obnoxious chirp. Her heart thudded so heavily in her chest she could feel the reverberation in her throat and temples.

Matt strode to his desk and he snatched up the receiver. "Hello?"

Dani caught her breath. She pressed the sleeping infant closer, praying softly, "Please don't let it be the Delaney sisters wanting Kyle back."

Matt's taut face eased into a relieved smile. "Well, hello, *Mrs. McAdams.*"

He met her gaze to gauge her response to his not so cleverly coded message. She shook her head violently. The last thing she wanted right now was a long talk with good old Mom.

Understood, Matt said with his empathetic brown eyes.

"Um, why no, ma'am, I haven't seen Dani. Shouldn't she be off on her honeymoon by now?" He paused, apparently listening to her mother's retelling of the story. "Then she didn't get married? And she's going to try to keep the baby?" He winked at her across the room. "Well, good for her. I hope she pulls it off."

"Oh, do you?" Dani squirmed deeper into the supple leather couch and it groaned.

"Yes. Uh-huh. I see." Matt leaned over the desk, putting the receiver as close to the phone base as possible. "If she does show up, I'll have her call you right away. Yes, and 'll do everything within my power to keep her from running off again. Goodbye.''

He dropped the handset in place as if it were a red-hot iron and swung his gaze to hers. Without missing a beat, he said, "We've got to get the hell out of here—now."

Chapter Three

Chapter Two

"Damn." Matt struck the heel of his hand against his steering wheel. He shook his head at the sight on the side of the secluded country road. "Of all the times to get a flat tire."

He pulled his four-wheel-drive vehicle in behind Dani's shiny red economy car and killed the engine. The humid afternoon air enveloped him as he hopped out of his Range Rover and approached her. "Looks like you need rescuing for the second time today."

She glanced down at the deflated tire. "Can you believe the luck I'm having?"

A light breeze sent a shower of cottonwood blossoms swirling between them. One of the pieces of white fluff lodged in the crumpled veil layered over her rich brunette hair. Matt reached up to pluck it away, smiling as he softly said, "You wouldn't be in this fix if you hadn't insisted we take two cars."

"We couldn't have fit the three of us and all our things in my car. And I didn't dare leave it parked in front of your house." She narrowed her flashing green eyes at him. "Do you have any idea what kind of scandalous talk that would have caused around town?"

She stood so close he could actually feel the rise and fall of her chest with each breath. His hands flexed in anticipation. How easily he could pull her to him. He looked down at her beautiful face. "Yeah," he croaked. "I can very well imagine the kind of conclusions folks would jump to."

She set her lips. "Then you see why we had to take two cars."

He inhaled the warm scent of her, setting his heart to hammer ruthlessly in his chest. He crossed his arms over his formfitting T-shirt, trying in vain to hold back his instinctive response to her nearness. "We could have dropped your car off at your house and loaded all that stuff into my car. That would have given you a chance to change, too."

She shook her head. Sunlight glinted off her dark curls. "There's a baby stroller, a Portacrib, two bags filled with clothes and toys, plus a case of diapers in my trunk. We didn't have time to reload all that and move the car seat or for me to change." She rustled the stiff skirt of her gown in one hand, then dipped her chin and lowered her voice. "Just like we don't have time to stand around rehashing things when we should be fixing that flat."

"We?" He grinned at her. "You plan on helping?"

"I'm certainly capable." She threw her shoulders back in a show of stubborn pride, thrusting the sun-brightened rise of her breasts close to his own chest.

Matt dipped his gaze to the inviting valley of her cleavage. "Honey, you're capable of all sorts of things, some of which you haven't even imagined." He swallowed hard and shifted in his suddenly too tight jeans. "But you're not dressed for changing a flat tire."

She cast her eyes downward. "That's the second time you've mentioned my dress. I can't help thinking that seeing me in a wedding dress has you a little bothered."

Yeah, hot and bothered, he thought, licking his lips. He tore his gaze from her body to meet her concerned gaze. He managed a fairly convincing laugh. "Why should it bother me?"

"Because I bought this dress to marry another man," she said all too softly.

Matt scoffed. "Obviously the guy didn't mean that much to you or you wouldn't have run out on him."

"I won't pretend I fell head over heels for Roger. Still, I think we could have had a nice marriage. But when he wouldn't accept my decision to adopt Kyle..." She stole a quick peek through the open car window at the baby sleeping peacefully in his car seat. "I had no choice. I had to leave Roger at the altar."

Matt's disappointment at her answer took him by surprise. What had he thought? That she'd throw herself into his arms and confess she couldn't go through with the wedding because of her undying love for him? He watched her as she checked on the baby, her face lit with a becoming maternal glow. He sighed. Thank God for little, diaper-clad miracles. If not for that baby, Dani would be married to someone else right now. The thought tore away at the fresh wounds of Dani's final rejection. But this was neither the time nor place to give in to an aching heart. He stiffened his spine and strode to the back of Dani's car.

"I need to get out the jack and spare tire," he said.

"The trunk key is in a magnetic box under the bumper." She pointed.

He reached under the car, asking, "Do you really think that's wise?"

She laughed lightly and moved toward him. "C'mon Matt. What's going to happen in Woodbridge, Indiana?"

"Obviously something." He straightened and held out his empty hand. "The key box isn't there."

"What?" Dani pushed him aside and bent low to peer under the car. She squinted and muttered something unintelligible, then suddenly brightened. "Here it is." She stretched her arm beneath the car and retrieved the small black box. "It wasn't in its usual place. Maybe the drive on the bumpy country road dislodged it."

"Maybe," Matt said, lifting his gaze from her to the smooth lane winding past where they stood. "And maybe you should just be more careful with your keys."

"Key." She slipped it from the box and held it aloft. "One key. To my trunk. No big deal." She rolled her eyes. "Jeez, Taylor, just because I asked for your help doesn't mean you have the right to get all protective on me."

"Fine." He closed the gap between them with one step.

"Fine." She shoved the key in his direction.

"I won't get protective." He put his hand over hers. The hot trunk key burned slightly against his palm but the feel of her skin on his singed him to his soul. He lowered his head until his world narrowed down to her searing green eyes. "Like hell I won't get protective," he whispered. "I wouldn't even be here if I didn't feel protective—of you and of Kyle. And I don't want you to doubt that, not for even a moment."

"I won't." She curled her slender fingers around his hand.

"Good." He fit his other arm around her waist and waited for her to resist.

She wet her lips and arched her back against the tightened muscles of his forearm. Her free hand clutched the clingy T-shirt fabric stretched taut over his back.

At first, he met her lips in a slow, tentative movement, allowing her the chance to break it off with both their dignities intact. But she didn't break it off. She moaned—

softly—but with enough eagerness to send thrilling vibra
tions skittering throughout his body, urging him on.

He pressed his mouth to hers, taking what had alway
been his. Putting on a white gown would not have made he
another man's bride, neither would enduring a meaningles
ceremony. This kiss, this claim, this joining meant she be
longed to him and him alone—just as surely as if they ha
vowed it so. And if it took forever, he would make her se
that, too.

He slicked his tongue over her parted lips, anticipating
deeper union. She gasped. Her fingers sank into the flexe
muscles of his shoulders. The tip of her tongue flicked ou
then withdrew. She flattened her palms, dragging ther
slowly around his body. When both hands rested on hi
chest, she gave a resounding shove.

She tore her lips from his. In the same instant one wor
ripped through the stillness of the moment. ''No.''

''No?''

''We can't.'' She stepped back. ''It's wrong.''

He moved toward her and laid his hand on her cheek. ''I
felt right to me.''

She shook her head, turning her lips to lightly brush hi
palm. ''No. It felt good to you. There's a difference.''

He wanted to correct her, to take her face in his hands an
kiss her again—this time so thoroughly she'd never agai
question how right it was. But he refrained.

''Oh, Matt.'' She sighed. ''So much has happened in th
last few weeks, I feel like my thoughts and emotions hav
been thrown into a giant blender and pureed.''

He dropped his hand to her shoulder and gave it an em
pathetic squeeze.

''This just isn't the time to toss another ingredient into th
mix.'' She raised her tear-dampened face to meet his gaze
''Do you understand that?''

He nodded.

"I know I can't tell you how to feel," she went on in a hushed tone. "Obviously I can't even get a handle on my own feelings."

He wanted to ask her to clarify that statement, but he held back. She didn't need the strain of having to explain herself to him.

Dani glanced down, took a deep breath, then lifted her gaze again. "But even if our feelings run totally amuck, we still have control over our actions."

Not so, he wanted to shout at her. With her eyes, she asked him to keep his peace. A sudden summer breeze whistled loudly in the silence. White puffs from the cottonwoods blew over them like a fragile first snow. Finally Matt sighed and nodded.

"Matt," she put her hand on his bare arm, "I can't afford the distraction of any physical involvement with you right now, can you understand that?"

"I understand." He glanced down at her hand on him, then squeezed his eyes shut. "I don't like it, but I understand."

"Good. Because I need you as a friend—now more than ever." She took the trunk key back from his grasp and pushed past him.

He overcame her, closing his hand on hers once more to retrieve the key. "What you're saying..." He hedged closer, fitting her body next to his. "Is that you want to keep things..." He eased the gleaming silver key into the unyielding lock. "Strictly platonic."

She held her body rigid against his. "Strictly."

"I'm warning you, that won't be easy for me." The lock clicked softly as he twisted the key. "When I'm near you, I still get those old familiar...stirrings."

"Well, you'll just have to deal with it." She placed her hand on the trunk to keep it from flying open. "Now could we end this discussion and get my tire changed?"

Matt held his hands up in a sign of surrender and backed away. She thanked him with a snappy nod, then gripped the trunk hood with both hands and raised it.

Immediately something in bright, translucent red leapt into her face. She shrieked. She stepped back, with a look of utter amazement, and the trunk sprang fully open. A rainbow of colors rose slowly around her. "How did these balloons get in my trunk?"

"Dumb question from a lady driving a wedding getaway car with a key hidden under the bumper." Matt laughed at the vision of Dani standing in a slow-drifting cloud of colors.

She blinked at him. "I made everyone promise not to decorate the car. I guess this is their revenge—filling my trunk with helium balloons."

"Um, Dani." Matt stuck his tongue in his cheek to keep from blasting out a belly laugh. "Those aren't helium balloons."

"Of course they are." She batted a sluggish oblong one away. "The heat from the trunk obviously subdued their buoyancy, but they're still helium balloons."

The wind picked up and whisked two long green ones out into the deserted country lane. A bright yellow one blew past Matt, missing his head by inches. He fought to keep his amusement under wraps as he focused his gaze on Dani. "I'm not arguing that they're filled with helium, I'm telling you they're not balloons."

She crossed her arms over her gown's white-beaded bodice. "Then what are they, smarty-pants?"

"Colored condoms."

The look on her face was priceless. She scanned the air around her. Each time her gaze landed on another elongated shape, her eyes grew wider. "Oh, my gosh, that's just what they are." She blushed and whirled to face Matt, her chin tilted up at a defensive angle. "Well, how was I supposed to know? I've only seen ... those ... in a theoretical setting, never as party decorations."

That revelation made his heart as light as, well, as the colorful shapes winding and bobbing in the breeze. Apparently old Roger hadn't been any more successful than he had in changing Dani's mind about waiting for the wedding night. "Well, you have to admit, it's an interesting choice."

Dani leaned back to allow a particularly lively red one bound past her at chin level. She stared at it for only a second before she burst into laughter.

Matt threw his arm around her and joined in. The frivolity played out quickly when Dani gasped, slapped him in the chest and clutched his arm. "Oh, my gosh. We've got to get them back."

"Why?"

"Why?" She ducked between his car and hers, heading onto the road where one hovered lazily. She called over her shoulder, "Because we can't be responsible for littering the countryside with ... those."

She had a point, he admitted. Grudgingly he bent down to scoop up the most lackluster of the bunch, which lay in the grass around the two vehicles. "But what are we going to do with them? They're not going to be easy to burst, and I don't happen to have a pin handy. We can't even put them into the trunk, we need to get in there."

"We'll put them in the back of your car."

"It's not a car," he instinctively protested, "It's a ..."

"I know, I know, it's a trophy. It's proof to the world that you're a bona fide success."

"I hardly need to prove anything to the world...."

"Maybe that is overstating things," she conceded, tucking one inflated condom under her arm.

"I should say."

"I, of all people, know the only people you care about impressing are the residents of Woodbridge. You want them to know you've risen above your upbringing."

The sympathy in her voice stung more than any sarcasm. He opened his mouth to deny her claims but she cut him short.

"Everyone in town is proud of you, Matt. Me most of all." She stood there for a moment, her eyes shimmering. Then, without warning, she straightened and brandished the elongated "balloon" in her hand. "But enough sentimentality, we have work to do."

She yanked open the door of Matt's Range Rover, shoved her catch inside, trapping them with a slam of the door. "We can dispose of these later, at the bed and breakfast."

She went chasing off after a blue one that seemed determined to lodge itself in the branches of a small tree. Matt grinned broadly when she, in full wedding regalia, leapt into the air to snag the prize. Much as he wished he could do the same to her—to grab her and hold her—he let it go. Only moments before she had dismissed any relationship they might have as a distraction, merely a physical involvement. After all they had shared, to settle for that would be unfulfilling at best.

Soon, the back of his Range Rover was filled with the colorful condoms. Try as he might to push them down out of sight, they kept floating up in full view through the big back windows.

Matt spent the next ten minutes wrangling all the baby things out of Dani's trunk while she stood beside the car with Kyle in her arms. The baby had awakened in a cranky mood, fussing quietly and refusing to be comforted by Dani's soft lullabies. Finally Matt tugged free the Portacrib. He leaned it against the car fender, then cupped his hand over Kyle's head. "How's the little trooper doing?"

Dani jiggled the infant on her hip. "I just changed him, so that can't be what's wrong. I think he's hungry, or else he's teething. Either way, the sooner we get where we're going, the better."

"Agreed." Matt squinted off in the direction of the setting sun. "We'll be on the road in a few minutes."

He stuck his head back inside the gaping trunk. The smell of car oil and new tire rubber greeted him. The textured tread burned against his fingertips as he pried the small tire from its well. He lifted the tire up, gave it a swift visual examination, then dropped it with a thud back into the trunk. "Your spare is flat, too."

"You're kidding."

"Believe me, not even I have that sick a sense of humor." He rubbed his hand over his aching neck. "Guess the only thing we can do now is load all this stuff into the four-wheel drive and head on. We'll come back for your car in the morning."

Reluctantly Dani agreed. As quickly as they could, they piled the baby's things, Dani's suitcase, the car seat and Kyle into Matt's brand-new Range Rover and started off for the bed and breakfast where Dani had reservations.

Half an hour later, Matt pulled into the allotted spot in front of a quaint Victorian farmhouse with a sign in front proclaiming Rosemont House.

Dani wasted no time in clambering out of the car when it came to a stop. After this harrowing day, all she wanted was to get Kyle situated, then sink into a hot bubble bath and escape from the pandemonium for a few minutes. She hurried around the car, thinking only of getting Kyle from his car seat. Gravel gouged her tired feet through her delicate wedding slippers. The hem of her once pristine gown swept up a thin, gritty cloud in the tiny parking lot. She rounded the bumper and ran smack dab into a thin older gentleman in denim overalls and a flannel shirt.

"Whoa, there, little lady." He caught her shoulders in his weathered hands and kept her from skidding into a fall.

Matt climbed out of the Rover and nodded to the man, then turned to open the back door.

"Looks like you're our honeymoon couple," the man observed. His eyes twinkled as he bounced his gaze from Dani's gown to the inflated prophylactics waving from the back window.

"We're..." She bit her lip and looked down. Matt's presence made the man's gentle teasing almost unbearable. In front of any other male on earth, including the man she had very nearly married, it wouldn't have been a problem. But Matt's nearness made her all too aware of the implications of the man's jest. Her heart stilled, racked with pain for the past, for the honeymoon that never was, the marriage that would never be.

Don't be foolish, she told herself, you have the baby and that's enough. She raised her head, determined to smile her way through the awkward moment, and lie like the devil.

She took a moment to compose some kind of answer while Matt pulled Kyle out of the car and came to stand beside her.

The older man raised one gray, bristled eyebrow and asked, "You *are* the honeymoon couple, aren't you?"

"Second honeymoon," Dani blurted.

Matt cocked his head in curiosity at the surprising response.

"I see." The man stroked his chin in a thoughtful gesture. "I'm Ed Rose. The wife and I own this bed and breakfast." He worked his jaw under his gnarled fingers. "Truth is, the mother of the bride..." He narrowed one eye at Dani. "She paid for the week's stay by credit card. Been holding the room under her name—so we weren't exactly sure who we were waiting for."

Dani pursed her lips once more, hoping another fabrication would spring forth from her frazzled mind. After all, she couldn't give her real name and have Mr. Rose wonder why her married name and her maiden name were the same.

"Taylor." Matt stepped forward and shot his hand out toward the curious older gentleman. "The name's Taylor. I'm Matt and this is Dani."

Ed Rose gave Matt's offered hand two hard yanks, looking more as though he was milking a cow than greeting a guest. The man trained his gaze on Dani again and nodded. "Welcome, Mrs. Taylor."

Mrs. Taylor. Dani Taylor. The very sound of the name shot tremors of excitement through her body. To keep herself from grinning like a sappy love-struck fool, she reached over and pulled Kyle from Matt's arms. "Our sitter canceled at the last minute, Mr. Rose. I hope bringing the baby won't be a problem."

He squinted at the wriggling child.

"We brought a crib," she added with a hopeful note.

Mr. Rose tipped his head back and studied the baby down the length of his long nose. "No," he said slowly. "It's not a problem."

Dani curled Kyle close. His little body went rigid and he turned his face away from her comforting shoulder. She let out a nervous laugh that she immediately wished would waft away on the evening breeze. She patted the baby's sweat-dampened back. "He's had a long day. If we could just get checked in . . ."

"Of course." Mr. Rose beckoned to them with his lean, curved fingers, then turned. He headed up the tulip-lined sidewalk that led to the welcoming front porch.

Dani started after him but Matt hooked his hand around her upper arm and held her back. "We'll just get our things and be right in, Mr. Rose," he called. When the older man was out of earshot, he loomed over her. "What was the idea of saying we're on our second honeymoon?"

Dani shrugged. "I just couldn't face trying to explain it all, Matt—the ruined wedding, my running away, the baby." She dropped her gaze from his intense brown eyes and concluded, "And bringing you along. I didn't want to have to justify it all right now. Saying we were on a second honeymoon alleviated all that."

"Granted, it did solve that problem, but it created a whole new one. One you may not have thought about."

"What?"

"As a married couple..." He lowered his face so close she could see the faint crinkles around his impish eyes, even in the fading daylight. "We really should sleep in the same room."

His warm breath bathed her cheeks. The kiss they'd shared earlier flashed through her mind. The memory, mixed with the import of his words, made her shiver. She wet her lips and opened her mouth to speak. At that precise moment, Kyle showed his discontent by emitting an ear-splitting screech. Matt jumped back, allowing Dani to examine the crying infant.

"Is he okay?" Matt asked.

"I think so—or at least he will be, when we get him fed and settled in for the night." She laid him on his stomach over her upper body and collected a diaper bag from the back of Matt's car. "I'm going to go on in. Can you handle the rest of the things?"

It took three trips, but Matt finally did get all of the suitcases and baby paraphernalia into the cozy bedroom they'd been given.

"That's the last of it," he announced, dropping his load at the foot of the bed. "How are things on this end?"

Dani looked up from the rocking chair the hosts had graciously moved into the room for the baby. In her lap, Kyle icked and squirmed and generally resisted the bottle she was trying to give him. "This end is at the end of her rope."

"You think it's the teething?" Matt squatted in front of them and caressed Kyle's flailing leg with his large hand.

Dani bit her lip and shrugged. Tears of frustration stung her eyes.

"Is there any medicine for a baby cutting teeth?"

"The little tube in the side pocket." She waved one limp hand at the bright blue bag he had just brought in. "The gel numbs his gums."

Matt dug the small white tube out and brandished it for her approval. She nodded. Or, at least, she meant to nod. But by now the effort was so monumental that all she managed was to slump her head forward a little.

"Okay, let's see if this helps." Matt covered the tip of his forefinger with the pinkish gel, then stuck it into Kyle's mouth.

The baby fought and squalled but Matt kept up the insistent rubbing until he quieted. Soon, Kyle let out a shuddering breath, then latched onto the bottle's nipple and began to suck noisily.

"Now you," Matt said, aiming his no-nonsense gaze at her.

"I don't think there's enough of that pink stuff to numb me in all the places I ache," Dani answered.

"No, but there is a big, beautiful claw-foot bathtub right through those doors." He helped her up, baby and all. "Maybe a hot bath will ease a few of those weary muscles."

She handed Kyle to him, pausing to plant a kiss on the baby's soft hair before she whispered to Matt, "Thank you."

Ten minutes later, she slid into a steamy, floral-scented bath. All the day's anxieties began to dissolve. The water lapped at her tired body in a soothing rhythm. The frothy bubbles clung to her sensitized skin, while the heat and oil in the blue water penetrated her exhausted muscles.

"I think I'm going to live in here for the next twenty-four hours," she called out to Matt through the closed door.

"And miss out on experiencing a beautiful June day in the Indiana countryside with Kyle?"

She smiled at that thought. A tingling inner warmth spiraled through her at the image of watching Kyle smell a flower for the first time, or seeing him reach his tiny hands out as a butterfly flitted over his curly blond head. She sighed. "Okay, Taylor, you win. I'll have to make do with only another half hour in here."

She shut her eyes and laid her head back against the cool, comforting porcelain lip of the tub.

"The little guy's getting sleepy." Matt's hushed voice reached her clearly, as if no door separated them.

Dani's eyes popped open. Her spine jerked rigid. She stared at the heavy door, painted glossy white. The antique glass knob shone back at her in testament that the door had not been disturbed. She had to shake her head at her own foolishness as she submerged herself once more in the warm blue water. She called back to Matt, "Maybe the baby will sleep through the night. He's had quite an adventure today."

"He's not the only one."

The tender tension in his tone touched her heart. She covered her eyes with her wet palms and said, "Have I told you how much I appreciate everything you've done?"

"Don't mention it," he said.

"Don't mention it?" A wry chuckle rattled through her tight chest. "You're certainly being an awfully good sport about this. Especially considering the circumstances, with me almost marrying Roger and all." A chill swept over her exposed arms and shoulders. She swallowed hard. Say something upbeat she told herself, something to get the conversation going again. She slicked her tongue over her dry lips, then uttered the first thing that sprang into her mind. "Really, Matt, I do appreciate your help. I don't know how I'm ever going to repay you."

Her words hit the tension-filled air like bacon on a hot griddle.

In the other room, Matt cleared his throat.

She wanted to say more. She opened her mouth but not a single syllable came to her rescue.

"I'll tell you how you can repay me." Matt's low, purposeful voice startled her. Again she looked up to make sure he wasn't standing inside the nearby doorway.

"How?" she asked, her gaze practically penetrating the closed door.

"Tell me why you ever accepted Roger Grant's marriage proposal."

Dani caught her breath. She looked down at the glittering engagement ring still circling the third finger of her left hand. On impulse, she tugged it off and dropped it onto the towels stacked beside the tub. Somehow, the action brought her tremendous relief. Contentment drifted up from her unburdened heart and raised the corners of her mouth in a lazy smile. "The answer to your question is very simple, Matt, very logical. So much so that you, or at least the lawyer part of you, will have to acknowledge the sheer perfection of it."

He coughed a derisive laugh, then he deadpanned, "State your case."

Dani filled her lungs with moist, floral-scented air. She could never have made this confession looking into Matt's eyes, but the door and the distance between them gave her a sense of freedom. "I agreed to marry Roger because we both wanted the same things—marriage, home, children— and we both wanted them *now*."

"I see," he said matter-of-factly. "Kyle's asleep. I think I'll put him down, then go for a quick walk."

She sat up fully. Water sloshed over the edge of the tub and dripped onto the white tile floor. "I see? That's it? No probing cross-examination?"

"Dani, I, of all people, should understand your motives. What else is there to say?"

Plenty, she thought, but it could wait. She shut her eyes and sank back into the tub. From the bedroom, she heard Matt murmur something to Kyle, then let himself out. She sighed. Maybe things would work themselves out after all. Maybe here, away from the chaos she had created in her life, with just Kyle and Matt to think of, she could finally regain her perspective. And why not? This was where she'd intended her new life to begin anyway. And though this wasn't exactly the life she'd envisioned, this was as good a place to start it as any. She smiled with excitement. A new life with a new baby. It couldn't get any better.

Yes, it could. Excitement turned to anticipation, and then to a deep-seated thrill radiating through her entire body. Could the twist of fate that brought Kyle to her have other things in store? She stared at the door, picturing the inviting bedroom beyond. She bit her lip and gripped the slippery edges of the tub until wet friction burned her palms. Whatever happened, she thought, this could well be the most pivotal week of her entire life.

Chapter Three

Matt paused at the door to the room and noted his reflection in the small brass knocker. He pushed one hand back through his windblown brown hair, releasing the scent of fresh air into the musty hall. His half hour walk had done nothing to clear his head. Now he had to go back in that room and project an aura of absolute confidence—and absolute control. Not an easy task for a man who wanted to demand to know where he stood, who wanted to lay the woman he loved down and pleasure her until the passion overwhelmed them both.

He glanced down at the basket of food and champagne that Mr. Rose had just given him. The single light in the hallway cast a warm yellow glow on the elegant array of fruits, crackers and cheeses. The perfect romantic repast. He thought of the room beyond the door with its four-poster bed covered in a thick quilted comforter and crystal vases filled with freshly cut flowers. The perfect romantic rendezvous. And he had to march inside and act, not like

Dani's lover, but like her friend, her staunch supporter, her lawyer.

If only it were that simple. If only he could think of all this as the trained, objective professional he knew himself to be. The image of Dani holding Kyle in her arms assaulted him. All hope of objectivity vanished. For her, he would do anything—including setting aside his own feelings for a time in order to concentrate on her needs.

He threw back his shoulders. Wary of waking the baby, he made three sharp metallic clacks with the knocker, then whispered, "Dani, are you decent?"

Soft shuffling noises answered him.

Had she heard him? He raised his voice slightly. "Dani?"

More shuffling. The sound of suitcase locks popping open.

"Hang on a minute, Matt." Dani's voice cracked mid-whisper.

Matt dutifully waited, shifting the laden basket in his arms.

The suitcase slammed shut. Dani muttered an unintelligible sound of frustration. Something fell to the floor with a thud. Matt opened his mouth to tell her he'd come back in a few minutes. Before he could form a word, the door swung open.

A breathless Dani stood in the doorway, her usually perfect hair a disheveled mess, her creamy cheeks tinged hot pink. Matt's gaze moved downward. Instantly he recognized his own red-and-black flannel shirt thrown haphazardly over her shoulders, its hem falling almost to her knees. The open cuffs dangled past her fingertips. They flopped back to expose her bare forearms when she raised her hands to pull the shirt closed over her nightgown.

White lace, red ribbons and black sheer fabric flashed through Matt's mind—images of the lingerie Dani had sworn she would wear for him on their honeymoon. His eyes focused on Dani's fingers fumbling to fasten a button, any button, on the shirt. Her movements gave him welcome glimpses of the unadorned pink gown she wore. Male pride swelled within him to see that she had chosen such a sweet, unimaginative gown for her initiation into the physical side of the marriage to Roger Grant.

He stepped inside the room and set the food basket on the foot of the bed, then turned to Dani. She continued to devote her full attention to the task of covering herself, without much success. Matt stifled a husky laugh. He moved to her. "Here, let me do that."

His fingers replaced hers on the lowest button of the shirt. "Your mother popped for the full honeymoon package. That included the basket of goodies."

Dani gasped and lifted her expectant gaze to him. "My mother?"

"When she made the reservations for this place," he prompted. He slid the button into the notch and shrugged. "Guess she didn't have a chance to cancel it when you..." He narrowed one eye pointedly at her plain pink gown. "Changed your plans."

Dani blew her breath out slowly. "Then she doesn't know I'm here."

"She does now." One by one, with utmost care, Matt worked his way up the shirt to the collar, then placed one finger under her chin and raised her face to his. "I left a message on her machine to let her know you're safe."

"Am I?" She swept just the tip of her tongue over her lower lip.

It was such an unconscious gesture that Matt wasn't sure she'd been aware of it. But Matt was aware. Dangerously aware. He recalled their earlier kiss. And just as quickly, her dismissal of his feelings as lingering lust intruded. From the corner of his eye he saw Kyle shift restlessly in the crib, then his gaze fell fully on Dani's mouth again. She pressed her hands to his chest and he wondered if she could feel the thrashing of his heart against his breastbone.

"Matt, tell me that I'm safe with you." Her green eyes pleaded with him for reassurances.

He curled his hands into fists at his sides, commanding his desire for her to quell enough to let him do the right thing. He tensed his jaw and let out a low, rumbling groan. It faded to a laugh. He placed a kiss on the corner of her pouting mouth. "You're safe with me, Dani. I promise."

She thanked him with her eyes—or was she scolding him? Knowing he couldn't afford to start speculating, he cleared his throat and nodded stiffly toward the basket. "How about an evening snack?"

"Great," she said with a touch of forced enthusiasm. "I haven't eaten all day. I'm starved."

"Then we'll make a picnic of it." He leaned over and snatched up the basket, lifting it for her inspection. "We have everything you could want, including champagne."

Dani reached out to trip her fingertips down the neck of the dark bottle. "Not the champagne, Matt. I don't feel much like celebrating."

"Okay." He gripped the bottle in one hand and swung it free in a definitive arc. "We'll save this for a toast on the day Kyle's adoption is finalized."

She smiled. "It's a deal. Now, what else is in that basket?"

Dani dived into the wonderful fare. Matt wrangled two glasses of cold milk from Mr. Rose. They spent the next hour nibbling at the rich delicacies and skirting any real issues. Finally Dani patted her filled stomach, then yawned.

Matt insisted on being the one to sleep on the floor and Dani only had the strength for a brief argument before she gave in. She helped him spread out the spare blankets, thanked him again for his help, then practically melted into the big, soft bed.

The next morning, she stole away to dress in the bathroom. She peeked at Kyle and found him in a relaxed baby sleep so deep she had to put her hand on him to check his breathing. The tiny rise and fall of his chest reassured her and she turned her attention to Matt.

The poor man looked so uncomfortable scrunched up on the flat-napped carpet with the blanket barely covering his long legs. Tearing her gaze from the intriguing sight of his well-muscled calves, she nudged him with the toe of her tennis shoe. "Why don't you get up in the bed and grab a little more sleep? I'm going downstairs for coffee and to mix up more formula for Kyle."

Matt grumbled something and pushed himself up from the floor. Feeling brazen, she delighted in the view of him clad only in his briefs.

The sight took her back to summers spent beside the Woodbridge community pool in the days before careers, commitments and biological clocks had come to define their relationship. Then, she and Matt had laughed and splashed and used rubbing in sun block as an excuse to prolong touching each other. A delightful sense memory seized her and she shuddered at the invisible perception of Matt caressing her body again. She placed her hand above the scooped neckline of her T-shirt. To her surprise, the skin under her palm was hot.

Matt tumbled into the bed and pulled the comforter up over himself. Dani sighed, lifting her hand to fan her face. If she crawled in that bed right now, no one, not even dead-to-the-world Matt, would know. She could curl up against his body, draw comfort from his strong arms for a moment, then slip away before he woke. She bit her lip and held her breath. A hazy shaft of morning sunlight highlighted Matt's disheveled brown hair. She took a step toward the bed.

Then reality intruded in the form of a gentle tapping on the door. Dani jumped. She tore her guilty gaze from Matt's body.

"Yes?" she said as she threw open the door. "Oh, Mr. Rose." Who else would it be? she chided herself for stating the obvious. "Is there a problem? I hope the baby didn't wake your other guests last night...."

"Nothing like that, ma'am," Ed Rose said, dipping his head in greeting to her. "You got a phone call." He thrust the handset of a cordless phone toward her. "It was your mother. I told her I'd bring the phone up and asked her to call back in five minutes."

"Thank you." She reached for the small gray phone.

He held it just out of her grasp. "But if you think the ringing will wake up your family..."

Dani didn't have to follow the man's line of vision to know he could see Matt sprawled in the bed and would reasonably assume she had spent the night beside him. Even the moment's illusion of being Matt's wife made a strange heat glow deep in her stomach. Protective of her privacy and Matt's, she edged the door almost closed. "That's all right, Mr. Rose, I'll take the call in here. Thank you."

He handed her the phone. "Just bring it downstairs when you're done." He turned and waved a hand over his shoulder. "Continental breakfast is served until nine."

She cradled the phone against her chest and tiptoed into the bathroom. She'd hardly had time to situate herself on the gleaming white tile floor when an electronic purring sound filled the room. "Hello, Mom?"

She sighed at the sound of her mother's voice on the other end of the phone line, even if anxiety had reduced the woman's words to hurried chatter. The minute her mother paused to take a breath, Dani leapt in, urging, "Slow down, Mom. I can't make heads or tails of what you're trying to tell me."

Dani let her head fall back against the glossy white wall and listened to her mother. She shut her eyes against the glare of sunlight refracted through the leaded glass window—secretly wishing she could as easily shut out the harsh details of her mother's story.

"Are you saying..." She pressed her spine to the cold, unyielding wall. "That Roger sought out the Delaney sisters before they left town and told them about my plans to keep Kyle?" She gripped the phone, her throat mimicking the tightening as she tried to squeak out, "On purpose?"

Blood rushed to her head, making her mother's response sound tinny and far away. But that did not diminish the impact of the information. Roger Grant had found a way to exact his revenge for leaving him at the altar. And his vindictiveness might well cost her the most important thing in her life. She tried to swallow. She struggled to get her breath. Her mother went on unfurling the horrible details of Roger's spiteful act, finishing with the most startling revelation of all.

"He what?" Dani leaned forward, hugging her knees to her chest like a hurt child. "He actually told you that he believes that when Kyle is with the Delaneys, where he belongs, I'll come back to my senses and marry him?"

How could he? The question stabbed her tender heart. She swung her gaze over the sparkling white floor without really seeing anything—until a brilliant glint caught her eye. She plucked up the engagement ring she had set beside the tub the night before.

Her mother's voice intruded again.

"What? No, I have no idea what I'm going to do now." The medium-size diamond winked in the unadulterated morning light. She bit her lip and stared at it. Too bad it wasn't a crystal ball so she could see the right course to take.

"Dani?" Muffled tapping accompanied Matt's soft voice.

She jerked her head up so fast, the taut muscles in her neck pinched. Ignoring the smarting twinge, she glanced down at the ring in her fingers, then back to the closed door. She lowered her voice to a hurried whisper, "I take that back, Mom. I do know what I'm going to do. I'm going to fight for my baby—and with Matt's help, I'm sure I can win."

She murmured a hasty goodbye, then clicked off the phone. Determination burned in her veins and chased away the muddle of emotions that had held her in frightened indecision. She leapt up from the floor to fling open the door. "Matt," she said, "we have a problem."

It was too early in the morning for Matt to fully comprehend the complex tale that Dani was spinning. On a normal morning, one where he'd gotten at least a couple of hours of honest rest, he would have handled it with no hesitation. But this morning, with his entire body stiffened from a night on the cold, unpadded floor? A night punctuated by Kyle's periodic cries to be fed, changed and have his gums massaged? This morning, he just couldn't grasp what she wanted of him.

His empty stomach grumbled. He winced and adjusted his bare torso as he attempted once more to understand Dani's crisis. "You want me to stop Roger from telling the Delaneys that you're adopting Kyle?"

"No, no." She crossed her arms over her soft cotton shirt. "It's too late for that. He's already told them."

He scored his crooked fingers through his scalp until it tingled and tried again to get a perspective on the situation. "Then what do you want me to do?"

"Devise a plan of action, Matt." She slapped the back of her hand into her palm.

The sharp smack startled the baby. Matt watched little Kyle endeavor to raise his head from the bunny-patterned baby sheets in his crib. The task seemed monumental to the nfant, even when his chubby arms and legs got into the act, writhing back and forth. He looked for all the world to Matt like a weak turtle trying to move across deep, shifting sand.

"You look about the way I feel, buddy," he said as he went and lifted the baby to his shoulder. Kyle blinked at Matt and promptly yawned in his face. Matt chuckled. He could get used to this "daddy" routine.

"Here, let me change him." Dani pulled the baby away, blessing his downy head with a shower of tiny good-morning kisses. She moved through the room, gathering diapers, talc and baby wipes, clinging to Kyle all the while. In short order, she turned away from Matt and went to work.

Even with her back turned, Matt could read Dani's intentions. The diapering was just a convenient excuse to get her hands on that kid. The news from her mother had Dani scared. And she was right to be so.

"Dani," he murmured, "what kind of action do you expect me to take?"

"Legal action." She doused the baby's dimpled bottom with fragrant white powder. Through the resulting cloud of fine dust, she fastened her insistent gaze on him. "I want you to do whatever it is you have to do to insure that Kyle will be my son."

"It's not that easy, Dani." Matt shook his head. "I can't manipulate the law or the courts to suit individual desires. I can only work within the framework. And right now, I don't even know what we're up against."

"How do you find out?" She jerked free the adhesive strips on Kyle's disposable diapers. "How soon would you know something?" She mashed the tape down and picked up the diapered baby. "When can you get started?"

Matt rubbed his dry eyes. His head was spinning from the events of the last twenty-four hours, from Dani's questions, and from his own raw emotions. He filled his lungs with baby-scented air, held it, then let it out slowly. "I could

start gathering information today if I were in Wood
bridge.''

"That means you can get into court first thing tomor
row, right?''

He rolled his eyes to the cream-colored ceiling. "Dani
maybe you've taken the buzz about my being a legal wizard
a bit too literally.''

"But you could rush the process, couldn't you?''

"I could,'' he admitted. "But that's not my style, Dani
I never go into court without being as fully prepared as I can
be. I'm not going to change that now.''

Dani's stance went brittle. Her green eyes snapped in fury
To her credit, she kept any remarks about him placing his
career before her needs to herself.

He raked a knuckle over his unshaven jaw. The whiskers
scraped his skin like coarse sandpaper but he repeated the
motion. "That doesn't mean I can't make your case top
priority. Just give me a minute to consider how I can rear-
range my schedule to accommodate it.''

If he were honest, he'd confess to her right now that he'd
canceled all appointments and postponed all court dates for
the next two weeks. That's about how long he thought it
would take him to get back on an even emotional keel after
losing Dani to Roger Grant. If she'd given him even a hint
that she still cared about him, Matt might have revealed his
secret. But as it was, his pride would not allow it.

He stroked his chin again. "Yes, I suppose I could juggle
a few things on the old calendar to make room for your
case.''

She cast her gaze down, but not before Matt glimpsed the
tears trembling on her thick lashes. "I appreciate that.''

Matt wanted to go to her, to take her in his arms and
swear that he would make it all work out for her. But that
would be a fool's promise and in the end might hurt her
more than the truth. He tipped his head back and laced his

rms over his naked chest, anchoring his feet a shoulder-
idth apart. Since he'd chosen to hold out for making her
ice the truth, he had a little more of it to impart. "There's
omething else you have to realize, Dani."

She put her cheek to Kyle's and folded him into her arms.
I have Kyle and you're going to see that I keep him. What
lse do I need to know?"

"You have to take Kyle back to Woodbridge now."

"Why?"

"Because the Delaneys may have gone to the police. They
ay have a warrant out for your arrest."

"Arrest?" She choked out a phony laugh. "Me? That's
idiculous. I have every right to have Kyle."

"You had the Delaneys' permission to have Kyle. Some-
hing tells me they'll want to withdraw that in light of the
ircumstances."

"I don't care." Kyle reared back as she spoke. He jolted
eflexively, then relaxed and gurgled at Dani. This time the
ears flowed freely as she searched the baby's face and said,
'He's my baby now and nothing on earth can take him from
le."

"Be reasonable, Dani." He stepped toward her, his arms
pen wide. "There are plenty of things on earth that can
ake Kyle from you, the courts and the cops just to name
wo. And you don't want to give any of them justification
o do so by your actions."

"B-but..." Her lower lip quivered.

He placed one hand on her back and one on Kyle's, then
lrew them both into the shelter of his embrace. She let go
hen, heaving ragged sobs against his collarbone. The
varmth of her tears dampened the skin of his chest and
eemed to Matt to penetrate straight to his heart. He sighed
nd placed a kiss first on Kyle's head, then on Dani's. "I'll
lo everything within my power to see that you two stay to-

gether. But you have to promise that you'll do what I say— starting with going back to Woodbridge.''

"I'll do anything, Matt." She clutched him, digging her fingertips into the uncovered flesh of his back. "Whatever it takes to keep Kyle, I promise I'll do it."

He drew her to him, well knowing the time would come when they might both rue the pledge they had just made.

Chapter Four

Dani slammed on the brakes and gritted her teeth as her little car slid to a stop just inches shy of the intersection. If she'd been going the tiniest bit faster, she'd have made it through on the yellow light. But, she reminded herself, if she'd been going any faster at all, she'd have breached all semblance of responsible driving.

"That would look great," she muttered, bracing her palms on the steering wheel and locking her arms straight. "I convince Matt to call in some favors and get a judge to arrange an emergency hearing for temporary custody of Kyle—then I get arrested for speeding on my way there."

Dani let out an exaggerated sigh and twisted her neck to release some of the tension collecting there. In doing that, her gaze fell on the astonished expression of the woman in the car next to hers. Suddenly she realized she'd been sitting at one of only two traffic lights in Woodbridge, blithely talking to herself. She cringed then shrugged at the woman, who immediately swung her gaze back to the stoplight.

From that point on, Dani kept her thoughts to herself. Not an easy task for someone whose mind and emotions were about as subdued as a Ping-Pong ball thrown in a tile shower stall. The light changed and she eased her car forward, trying to concentrate on driving and not on what lay in store at the courthouse.

She squinted down the two-lane main street of town but did not see Matt's dark green Range Rover. How had he ever talked her into letting him take Kyle and going on to town ahead of her? She'd done it, she realized, because she had promised to abide by his decisions regarding the custody case. And this morning, Matt had drawn the conclusion that Dani should not be seen carting Kyle all over the countryside—even if she was trying to return the child.

Even *if*. Dani huffed. Matt's unnatural emphasis on that word still rang in her ears. He'd all but accused her of scheming to spirit the baby away to keep the Delaney sisters from taking him. She angled her car into a parking spot on the deserted town square, then sighed. She hated to admit it, even to herself, but Matt was right. The thought of putting Kyle into her car and driving as far away from Woodbridge as possible had crossed her mind.

She checked her watch: 2:05. The judge had asked that they convene in his chamber at two-thirty. Where was Matt? She craned her neck to look north, in the direction of Matt's home, then south, the direction Matt would arrive if coming from his law office. Bright June sunlight glinted off a windshield, stinging Dani's already weary eyes. She lowered her head to escape the discomfort.

Head bowed, she took a moment to utter a brief prayer that all would go well in court, finishing just as a car door shut with a heavy thunk right beside her. She jerked her head up to see a flash of forest green as a second door opened.

She wasted no time jumping out of her car and running around to help Matt take Kyle from his car seat. She rushed in between the two vehicles, intent on reaching the baby. But a very real, very intriguing obstacle stopped her.

Her mother would have had a fit to catch Dani staring with undisguised interest at Matt's muscular backside as he bent to retrieve Kyle from inside the car. Obviously there were times when mother didn't know best. She smiled to herself and bit her lip, using Matt's distraction over his task to allow her to slip up behind him.

"Need any help?" she asked, leaning so close she could feel the stiff fabric of his dress pants through her light-weight summer skirt.

Matt stilled. Only his head moved to put him in position to make eye contact. His inviting mouth curled into a sly smile. "I think I can manage to get one little baby out of one basic car seat. But if it stumps me, I'll holler."

Dani reached over and pinched the tight skin just above his belt line.

"Ouch!" Matt swatted her menacing fingers.

"You hollered?" She edged closer, her hands spread out to take the baby.

Matt pulled Kyle free from the car seat and straightened, keeping his back to Dani. "Look, Dani," he said over his shoulder as he fit the baby against his chest. "I know you want nothing more than to share a quiet snuggle with the baby, but it just isn't prudent. Not right now."

Dani shrank back from him, her hands falling limply to her sides. "Why?"

"Because Sarah and Veronica Delaney may show up at any minute. Can you honestly think of anything that might incite them more than to see you cooing and cuddling over the baby they feel is theirs?"

"He's not theirs." Hot tears burned above her lashes. "They don't even care—"

Matt whirled around to cut her off with a stern glare. "You promised to play this my way, Dani."

"B-but..." Her lip thrust out and quivered.

"No arguments." He backed his command up with an unyielding expression. "Either you follow my game plan or we don't play at all."

She swallowed. Or at least she tried to swallow, but her throat felt blocked, her air passages constricted. The blazing afternoon sun reflected off their two cars. It illuminated the golden highlights in Matt's warm brown hair. Still, the ice in his eyes remained.

Above the dull sound of her own heartbeat and the subtle sounds of Kyle sucking his pacifier, Dani heard another car draw close, stop and the engine cut off.

"What's it going to be, Dani?" Matt raised one eyebrow in an impatient challenge. Not far from them, two car doors opened and shut simultaneously.

"Okay." She lowered her gaze. "Whatever you think is best, Matt."

The voices of Sarah and Veronica Delaney clashed in hurried conversation. A deeper, masculine voice interrupted and a moment of frantic whispering ensued.

Matt turned and stepped in toward Dani, creating an intimate zone in which they could talk. "I have to know I have your cooperation on this before I go in there."

She nodded, her gaze wholly transfixed on Kyle's sweet profile.

"Because I truly believe we can win this first round if we play it right."

She looked up to meet Matt's intent eyes. "Really?"

"Yes." He smiled slightly. "And there are two reasons for that. One—" he held one long finger up "—in both our dealings with the Delaney sisters, they have been boorish, selfish and demanding." The women raised their voices.

Again, the male voice interceded. Matt shook his head. "I doubt they'll behave any better today."

Suddenly the pieces of Matt's plan locked together for Dani. "In contrast, if I'm compliant, helpful and show my concern for Kyle's welfare, that will count in my favor."

"Exactly." Matt's smile grew and she even detected a twinkle in his eye now. "And the second reason I think things may swing your way, is that the Delaneys live in Ohio. Obviously out of our court's jurisdiction. So, unless or until they succeed in getting the proceedings moved . . ."

"The judge will want to keep Kyle close by." She clapped her hands together.

Matt held his index finger to his lips to tell her to keep quiet. He glanced around to see if Sarah and Veronica had taken any notice of them huddled between Dani's car and his.

"Hey, Taylor." Wayne Perry, an old friend and legal colleague of Matt's waved and smiled broadly at him. He excused himself from the company of the dueling Delaneys and strode toward Matt with his hand outstretched. "Good to see you, man."

"Hello, Wayne." Matt gave his best no-nonsense handshake. He cocked his head toward Dani. "You remember Danielle McAdams, don't you?"

"Sure." He shook Dani's hand enthusiastically. "Sorry to meet you again under these circumstances but it couldn't be helped." He lifted his thin shoulders almost up to the ends of his shaggy blond hair. "The ladies needed a local lawyer, pronto, and it was suggested I take the case by another very influential client."

He glanced at Dani, winced, then gave an awkward chuckle probably meant to pass as an apology. "Roger Grant's business is the cornerstone of my practice."

She dropped her gaze for an instant. A red tinge washed over her face. She heaved a heavy sigh, then lifted her chin and donned a kind smile. "I understand."

"And this must be the little rascal that's causing us all to work on this beautiful Sunday afternoon." Wayne placed his hand on Kyle's back.

The infant responded by arching his spine and suckling faster on the red plastic pacifier. From the corner of his eye Matt could see Dani flatten her palms to the sides of her skirt. His heart ached to know how desperately she wanted to touch the baby herself. How bad could it be to let her stroke the baby's head or kiss his plump cheek, Matt wondered. Surely the Delaneys wouldn't begrudge her offering an innocent child some comfort in a distressing time. He shifted Kyle to his other shoulder, thinking to ask Wayne if there would be any objections to allowing Dani to hold Kyle during the hearing.

"There he is...."

"That precious, precious child."

Sarah Delaney rushed toward them, her hands flapping like an excited bird's wings. Veronica's approach was more subtle, her eyes focused with a calculating glint on little Kyle. They looked for all the world to Matt like vultures descending on a tempting morsel.

But this was one morsel that the vultures weren't going to get at. Not if he could prevent it.

"Excuse me, ladies." He capped Kyle's small head with one hand and turned his shoulder to protect the child from the grasping hands of Sarah. "But in light of the situation, I'll have to ask you not to handle the child."

"Why not?" Sarah Delaney, a woman in her early forties with a heavy hand for makeup, pointed her surgically sculpted chin at Matt. "He's our only cousin's child, our flesh and blood, our legal ward."

Matt heard Dani gasp and felt her tense. Before she could blurt out anything that might incriminate or discredit her, he wedged his body between her and the Delaneys. "That's not necessarily true, Ms. Delaney."

Veronica, the younger and more beautiful of the two sisters, raised one perfectly plucked eyebrow at him. "Are you saying Kyle might not be a Delaney by blood?"

Was that hope he heard beneath her flat midwestern accent? Matt wondered. "Um, no, Ms. Delaney." He studied Veronica's composed features for any betrayal of her real feelings about the child. "I have no reason to question Kyle's paternity, but whether or not you or your sister are his legal guardians..." He gave her his best witness-intimidating smile. "Well, that's what we're here today to decide, isn't it?"

"Mr. Taylor is right, ladies," Wayne interjected. He lifted his arm and twisted his wrist until the sun flashed off his gleaming gold watch. "And it's time we got inside."

Wayne ushered the two women around to the sidewalk, which led to the courthouse. As Matt watched them go, he debated which he found more grating, the clatter of their high heels on the pavement or their incessant bickering with each other.

Kyle wriggled and broke his musings. He glanced down at the guileless face and fathomless blue eyes of the baby whose fate rested in his own hands. A strange pang struck his heart and in that instant he knew just how Dani felt about Kyle—and how imperative it was that they win custody.

After giving Dani a last minute briefing about the proceeding, Matt placed his hand on her back to escort her inside. The marble corridors of the courthouse seemed especially cool in contrast to the summer heat.

"If I'd known the air-conditioning would be turned up full blast, I'd have brought an extra blanket to wrap around the baby," he said, trying to occupy Dani's mind with incidental things.

"You always accused me of being too warm-blooded," she said quietly. "Maybe if I held him . . ."

They rounded a corner and the judge's chambers loomed ahead of them. Beside the dark wooden door, Matt's secretary, Mrs. Lentz, stood talking to another woman.

Dani froze in her tracks. "What's my mother doing here?"

Matt's secretary moved to one side and Dani's mother noticed the two of them approaching. "Hi, sweetie. Hi, Matt. Are you ready for this?"

"What's she doing here?" Dani demanded again through a phony smile aimed right at her mother's cheerful face.

Matt leaned close and nudged Dani to get her walking again. "I thought we might need her as a character witness."

"Character witness?" She took a faltering step and then another. "You said this was an emergency hearing. That there wouldn't be any witnesses called. That you and the other lawyer would simply state our cases. That even I wouldn't have a chance to speak."

Matt patted Kyle in a soothing cadence when, in fact, it was Dani he wished to placate. "Don't let yourself get too worked up right now. Your mom is here as a precautionary measure."

They reached the waiting women. Dani's mother stretched out her arms and enclosed her daughter in a comforting embrace. Dani went rigid, her expression shifting from surprise to panic as her words rushed at Matt. "You think I don't know you've involved my mom because you want her to be here for me in case I lose custody of Kyle?"

"I wanted to be here for you—either way, sweetheart," Gwen McAdams said to her daughter. She grabbed Dani by the shoulders and shook her firmly. "Now pull yourself together. Don't make Matt's work any harder than it already is.''

Dani relaxed a bit and brushed a kiss to her mother's cheek. "I'm sorry, Mom, it's just that . . .''

"I know, dear, I know.''

Matt handed Kyle to Mrs. Lentz, then turned and knocked sedately on the door. A deputy sheriff wearing a gray uniform and a big golden badge stuck his head out. "The judge is running late. But you and your client can come in and sit.''

Dani heard the door shut behind her with finality. Matt helped her into a seat facing a dark desk, which overpowered the bland room. Her mother sat directly behind her and Matt's secretary, holding Kyle, sat next to the door in a folding chair. Suddenly it dawned on Dani that this was very probably a folding chair brought in for her would-be wedding the day before. She wound her fingers together tightly in her lap.

Matt settled into the chair to her left and she leaned over to him, whispering, "Evan Harcourt was the judge who almost conducted my marriage ceremony yesterday, Matt. Why did you allow him to hear this case?''

"I didn't allow anything. I took what I could get.''

She slumped back in her chair. She could practically feel the hope seep out of her spirit and the energy to face the judge drain from her body.

"Cheer up.'' Matt smoothed the side of his thumb down her cheek. "Judge Harcourt is an honest, fair, decent human being. We'll get an impartial hearing.''

She nodded glumly.

"And for what it's worth . . .''

She bit her lip and raised her gaze to his.

"I happen to know that Harcourt joined your mother and a few family friends in a congratulatory toast at the nonwedding reception.''

She sat up and opened her mouth but before she could ask any one of the dozen questions that invoked, the deputy strutted in and heralded the judge's arrival.

Evan Harcourt blustered into the small room, dabbing at the sweat on his bald head with a white kerchief. "Rushed all the way over," he said, his ruddy cheeks puffing out as he spoke. "Damn those sand traps anyway." He spanked away a dusty patch on the knee of his yellow-and-lime-green plaid golf pants. He plopped into the oversize chair behind the huge desk and zeroed his gaze in on Dani. "Well, hello again."

Her lips formed a hello but her voice deserted her.

The judge, in turn, greeted each of the parties involved in the hearing. Everything after that was nothing more than a blur of legalese to Dani.

"Pursuant to the matter of..."

She tried to concentrate but the only thing that seemed real to her in the whole room was the gentle sound of Kyle rousing occasionally in his sleep.

"The party of the first part..."

Kyle popped the pacifier out of his mouth. It dangled from his lips. Dani had to restrain herself to keep from leaping up and catching it. At the last minute, the baby drew the pacifier back into place. Kyle sighed in contentment and Dani sighed with him.

"As designated in the aforementioned codicil, dated..."

When would this ever end? What was she thinking? What if it did end but cost her Kyle? In that case, what could she do to drag it out as long as possible?

"Dani?" Matt curved his hand over her shoulder. She startled. "Dani, the judge asked you a question."

"Huh?" The room spun. She glanced down to steady herself. A reassuring squeeze from Matt anchored her once again in reality. She gave him a tentative look, pleading for help. "I'm afraid all the legal terminology has my head reeling."

Matt nodded and smiled. "Well, to put it succinctly, Judge Harcourt sees justification in both ours and the two Ms. Delaneys' petition for custody."

Judge Harcourt coughed. "Ms. McAdams, in considering this case, I am charged with seeing to the child's welfare as well as honoring the wishes of the deceased couple."

"Karen and Bill," she supplied almost inaudibly. It seemed so cold not to speak of them by name.

Judge Harcourt scowled, scanned a paper in front of him and then shrugged. "Yes, yes. Karen and Bill Delaney. In deciding where to place their surviving infant son, it is my responsibility to give adequate weight to the wishes expressed in their will."

That sounded good, as if the scales of justice might be tipping to their side. She straightened in her chair. "Yes, sir, I see."

"Those wishes allow me three choices," the judge continued. The bags beneath his benevolent eyes crinkled as he squinted at her. "To place the baby with his blood relatives, two women who have more than adequate economic resources to provide for him, two homes and access to the best child care money can buy."

Dani caught her breath and held it.

"Or to entrust him to an extremely busy young bachelor." He dropped his gaze over Matt and frowned. "A fine, capable and dedicated young man, to be sure. One who could meet the financial obligations and who lives in a fine new house, but who lacks any real experience in caring for an infant."

She grit her teeth and knotted her hands in her lap.

"Or I could place the child with you." He dipped his head toward her. "A charming young woman with pediatric nursing credentials, but one whose earning potential is limited by the economic realities of working in a small, financially strapped hospital. And one who is still living with her widowed mother, if I'm not mistaken.''

Dani shut her eyes and sighed, letting her heavy nod affirm the judge's assessment.

''I can't help thinking—'' Judge Harcourt stroked his round cheek with his thumb ''—that you and Mr. Taylor make a better case for custody as a team. After all, between the two of you, you could offer the child the home, care and financial security that you can't give him separately.''

Dani's heart flip-flopped. The man was advising—no, he was all but blackmailing them into—marriage.

Matt jerked his head up. ''Are you suggesting what I think you are, sir?''

''Why not?'' The judge chuckled heartily. ''As I recall you two were involved up until...a few months ago. In fact, weren't you engaged?''

Matt started to reply but Dani interceded. On top of all the insanity she had suffered today, she would not bear the indignity of hearing him candy-coat the most painful period of her life.

''No, Judge Harcourt, we were never officially engaged.'' She lowered her lashes to flash an accusatory glance at Matt.

''We had an understanding,'' Matt explained to the startled judge.

''No, you had an understanding—an understanding patsy in me,'' she muttered, trusting the rest in the chamber could not hear.

''You're saying then, that you were not engaged? That your long-term relationship was not marriage bound?'' The judge puffed out his cheeks and rumpled his brow at them.

''Ms. McAdams never had cause to doubt that my intention was to marry her, Your Honor,'' Matt said, his tone so hot Dani could almost feel steam rising from his blatant gaze on her face.

She drew a deep breath. "Your Honor, I never accepted Mr. Taylor's engagement ring or his proposal. I'm only trying to give an honest response to your question."

"Oh, by all means, be honest, Ms. McAdams." The judge grinned and strummed his fingertips on the desk like a child delighting in the antics playing out before him.

"As long as we're being perfectly honest, Your Honor, I never technically proposed to Miss McAdams." Matt faced forward, letting only a quick shift in his eyes betray the true target of his barbed remark. "However, I suppose one might construe that I did offer her a ring."

"Offer?" Dani placed her hands on her hips, her mouth dangling open. Matt kept his eyes straight ahead. Fireworks exploded inside Dani's chest. Her skin burned with fury. She zeroed in on the judge's obviously amused face. Her rational thought told her to hush, but she'd held in this particular pain for too long. It spilled out in a rush of words. "You're an expert at assessing situations, sir, would you call this offering me a ring? He took me out, ordered champagne, gave me roses, really built my expectations up—then accepted a phone call from a client."

"It was a crucial case, sir," Matt interjected.

"Then you should have excused yourself or called him back," Dani blurted out. "But no, you had to take the call at the table. And to top things off, the whole time you spoke to the guy, you had a ring box in your hand, waving it around, gesturing with every point you made."

Matt had no defense for his actions.

Again, Dani turned to the judge. "Everyone in the restaurant snickered, Judge Harcourt. I've never been so humiliated."

Matt bowed his head guiltily.

"He had his chance, Your Honor, to show me in that one symbolic moment just how he felt. And *did* he ever show me." She choked back the temptation to cry. "It was clear then that work came first." She jerked her face up and narrowed her eyes. "I ran out of the restaurant—without the engagement ring."

"I see." The judge pursed his lips in a pudgy frown. "Then, you had intended to marry each other, but a lover's tiff came between you?"

Dani blinked. "A tiff?"

"That may be simplifying things, sir," Matt said.

"Simplifying things is part of my job, Mr. Taylor." Judge Harcourt chuckled. "And from my vantage point, you two young people have excellent qualifications to care for the child and you have a long-standing relationship that only lacks a certificate to validate it."

"As a married couple?" Matt asked the judge.

"And why not? You're already fighting like one."

The small contingent in the room tittered with restrained laughter.

Dani straightened, struggling to make sense of what had just happened. Matt stood motionless.

The man must have interpreted their stunned silence for encouragement. He sat back, rubbed his well-padded palms together and grinned like a drunken Cupid. "And if you're amenable to the notion, I can arrange to waive the three-day waiting period and perform the ceremony myself tomorrow morning."

Judge Harcourt cocked his head. The overhead light winked off his bald spot. "Just a matter of a couple of details, really."

Matt shifted in his seat. "Details, sir?"

"No use pretending we don't all know that Ms. McAdams just had a blood test." The judge's face sobered.

"So granting her an exception to the three-day rule is no problem. But as for you, Mr. Taylor..."

Matt glanced at Dani and offered a bewildered shrug before responding to the judge's implied question. "I had an insurance physical last month, sir, with full blood tests."

"Lot can happen in a month, son." The judge narrowed his eyes at Matt. "Would you be willing to swear that since having those tests run that you've done nothing to put yourself at risk of contracting a..." He cast an embarrassed look at Dani, then finished his sentence with a brusque cough. "Social disease?"

"A...?" Matt scowled. He glanced around the room. Even the Delaney sisters fell into total silence.

Dani knew it was none of her business what Matt had done since their breakup over six months ago. Still, she found her pulse fluttering and her ears straining as she awaited his answer.

"Well, what do you say, son?" the judge demanded.

"Um, no, sir," Matt stammered.

A crushing weight settled in Dani's chest.

"I mean, yes," Matt corrected. "That is, no, I haven't done anything to put me at risk and yes, I can swear to that."

The dull pressure in Dani's chest eased, but it did not leave. This nightmare was far from over.

"Good. That will give me a local placement for the child." Judge Harcourt pounded his fist as though it were a gavel on the desk. "So, are we all set?"

The judge gazed at the two of them.

Dani's gaze fell to the floor.

Matt stared at her—a determined glare that forced her to raise her eyes to his.

Say something, Dani begged in silence. Say whatever it takes to get me Kyle so we can get out of here. She put her hand on his, hoping to prod him into saying some absolutely brilliant thing that would save the day.

Matt's mouth crooked up on one side. He sighed, then turned away from her. "We're all set, Judge Harcourt."

"We are?" Dani's hand convulsed over Matt's long fingers.

"We are," Matt whispered to her. His smile froze. He summed up the situation for her through his clenched teeth. "Dani, the judge is saying he's willing to give us custody of Kyle—at least for the time being—but only as a married couple. Do you want me to tell him 'no dice'?"

Dani shifted her eyes. Judge Harcourt beamed down at her and Matt, obviously quite pleased with his proposed solution. Her tender heart ached, her feet scuffed the floor as if to run away. Behind her, Kyle gurgled and she knew what she had to do.

Marriage. To Matt Taylor. She looked into his eyes. What did she see conveyed there? Affection? Yearning? Horror? She couldn't tell. Her heart skipped. She gulped down her own mixed dose of fear and excitement. Was this the lesser of two evils or the best of both worlds? There was no time now to sort it out.

She swallowed hard and tipped her chin up. "I think Matt and I would make excellent partners, um, parents, Judge Harcourt. I mean . . ." She glanced at Matt for help.

"She means, she's willing to give me the answer to the question I intended to ask in that restaurant months ago." He took her hands. His eyes sparked but his smile seemed tinged with sadness as he finished his statement. "Danielle McAdams has agreed to be my wife."

Chapter Five

"Do you, Danielle Olivia McAdams, take this man to be your lawfully wedded husband? To have and to hold from this day forward, in sickness and in health, forsaking all others, until death do you part?"

Matt held his breath and waited. Yesterday afternoon, when Dani agreed to this unlikely solution, he would have bet she would never see it through. Had he been wrong?

"I do." The simple words filled the nearly empty judge's chamber.

"Matthew Thomas Taylor, do you take this woman to be your lawfully wedded wife? To have and to hold from this day forward, in sickness and in health, forsaking all others, until death do you part?"

Matt gazed down at Dani's glowing face with relief. Funny, he thought, he'd imagined this moment more than once during their courtship—but it had never looked like this. He'd envisioned a big church wedding with half the town in attendance, not a judge's chambers with only Dani's mom and his own secretary as witnesses. He'd pictured Dani in an intricate white dress coupled with a white lace veil, which he would lift at the end of the ceremony to give her their first kiss as husband and wife. Instead she wore a simple floral print dress and a floppy hat, pinned up in front with a pink rose.

In those detailed notions of the "big day," Dani had always carried a huge fragrant bouquet of gardenias and orange blossoms. He dropped his gaze to little Kyle nestled happily in Dani's arms. Warmth washed over him. As amusing as those other wedding daydreams had been, nothing in his imagination could rival this moment for perfection. He felt his mouth broaden into a smile around his answer to the judge's question. "I do."

"Then, by the power vested in me by the state of Indiana, I now pronounce you husband and wife."

Husband and wife. The enormity of their action hit Matt full force. Danielle McAdams was now Danielle Taylor. He stared into the distance without seeing a thing while he tried to make that onetime fantasy a part of his reality.

Judge Harcourt coughed. Matt startled from his reverie and gaped at the man, who gave him a curt nod.

Matt responded in kind, blinked, then threw in a muttered thank-you as an afterthought.

"You're welcome, son." The judge jerked his head to Matt's left to indicate Dani.

"Um, she thanks you, too," Matt murmured.

Beside him, Dani giggled.

He glanced at her and noticed her cheeks were scarlet. In fact, her whole face had an amazingly attractive flush. Her vivid green eyes focused on him, then almost immediately her eyelids fluttered and her gaze plummeted. She sank her even white teeth into the full center of her sensual lips and...

Her lips. The kiss. Matt felt like kicking himself. But he felt more like doing what was expected of him—kissing the bride.

Careful not to squash Kyle between them, Matt took Dani by the shoulders and leaned over her. His mouth fit hers and that old familiar gratification flowed through his being. Instinctively he flicked his tongue out to tease the gentle parting of her lips. She answered with her own tongue and another all-too-familiar response welled up in his snug-fitting dress trousers. Judiciously Matt ended the kiss and eased Dani away from him.

Their gazes remained locked in a tender tangle of unspoken emotion even as they moved apart. The moment the couple separated, the women witnessing the proceedings cheered. Dani smiled shyly up at him. He wanted to tell her how happy he was that this day had finally come, even if only in pretense. He smoothed one hand down her arm, stepped closer, opened his mouth—and almost choked.

"Mom, please." Dani tried to shield Kyle from the shower of rice raining down on them.

Matt tried as inconspicuously as possible to spit out the stray grains that he had nearly swallowed.

"Now see here, Gwen McAdams," Judge Harcourt bellowed. "This is no place for that folderol."

"This is the only place for it, Evan," she argued, tossing her last handful. "As the town veterinarian, my late husband spearheaded the drive for a city ordinance prohibiting the throwing of rice on the courthouse grounds. It's bad for the birds and makes a mess on the sidewalk."

"What about the mess in my chambers?" the judge demanded.

She waved her hand to dismiss his complaint. "I'll come back and clean up every last bit of it. Right after I see these two off on their honeymoon."

She linked arms with Matt and Dani and beamed. In a matter of minutes, they, Dani's mother and Matt's secretary were standing on the curb outside the courthouse.

"Are you sure you don't want me to take the baby? Not even just for tonight?" Mrs. McAdams asked.

"No, Mom." Dani plopped Kyle's tiny baseball cap on his head, adjusting the brim to shade his eyes from the morning sunlight. "If you took Kyle it would defeat the purpose of everything we've accomplished here today."

"Well, not *everything*." Mrs. McAdams nudged Dani with her elbow and sent Matt an overplayed wink.

"Oh, Mother!" Dani suddenly became totally absorbed in situating Kyle's clothes.

"Well, all right then." The older woman sighed and shrugged. "If that's the way you want it."

"That's the way I . . ." She tugged at the round collar of Kyle's yellow T-shirt. "Matt and I . . ." She fidgeted with the blue buttons on his bright red overalls. "That's how we want it, Mother."

"Fine." She patted Dani on the back. "At least you'll have a lovely place to stay." She reached into her enormous purse and pulled out a manila envelope. "Here's some information on things to do in the area. I paid for the full week at the Rosemont House in advance, so outside of food and shopping, you shouldn't have any expenses."

"That's too extravagant, Mrs. McAdams," Matt said.

"Nonsense. Dani's father left me well taken care of."

"Thanks, Mom." Dani accepted the envelope, then leaned over to kiss her mother on the cheek.

"You have the number in case a client has an emergency or if there's any development in the custody case?" Matt asked his ever-efficient secretary.

"Yes, sir, and I've changed the message on your answering machine so folks will know you won't be back in the office until Monday."

"You're a jewel." He gave the gray-haired woman a peck on the forehead, then strode over to the Range Rover. Dani had already gotten Kyle into the car seat in the back. He considered walking around and opening the passenger door for his new bride, but when he closed in on her, she gasped, then bolted like a nervous colt. She had the door open and shut before Matt knew what to make of her reaction. He shrugged it off and before long they were on the road.

The silence in the interior of Matt's vehicle piqued Dani's already frazzled mind. Every ounce of self-control she possessed hardly kept in check the emotions and impulses raging within her. She clenched her jaw to contain the string of trite, schoolgirl phrases that wanted to gush from her lips. She rolled the large envelope her mother had given her into a tube, let it uncoil, then wound it up again—all to occupy her hands. Otherwise, she feared, they might reach for Matt—*for her husband*—and do something downright foolish, like slip through his thick brown hair. Or worse.

She dipped her gaze discreetly. Matt shifted his foot from the gas pedal to the brake and then back to the gas. The lean muscles of his thigh strained against the smooth fabric of his gray slacks. She curled the envelope tighter and tighter. She let her gaze wander ever so slightly off course and found herself contemplating her new husband's lap. She gripped the paper cylinder in her hands and a soft groan escaped her lips.

"Did you say something, Dani?" Matt kept his eyes fixed ahead.

Dani looked down at the slender tube in her hands and gasped. She let go of the rolled envelope as if it were on fire. It relaxed to its flattened state and she laid her head on the back of the seat. "I didn't say a thing, Matt." She shut her eyes. "Not a thing."

"Your eyes tired?"

She sat up. "Why would my eyes be tired? What do you think they've been doing?"

Matt cocked his head. "Calm down, will you? I was only trying to make conversation."

Conversation. Dani remembered how to do that, didn't she? She pressed her spine to the seat, then pulled her hair around to fall over one shoulder. She examined the deep brown strands as she tried to sound casual. "You'll have to forgive me, Matt. I'm still kind of jumpy."

"Who isn't?" He chuckled.

She plucked a ragged wisp of hair from the mass of curls. "It'll be good to get to Rosemont House and just relax and take it easy for a while."

"I can't wait. A beautiful spot away from our normal lives, with no small town gossip, no daily stress, no briefs."

She glanced up and raised an eyebrow.

"I meant legal briefs."

She couldn't help but smile. "I knew that."

He returned her smile twofold. "I'm looking forward to this week."

"Week?" She let her hair drop. "Can you really leave your practice for that long?"

He adjusted his shoulders and his suit jacket rasped against the upholstery. "Yes, I can leave my practice that long. Believe it or not, I've changed some in the past six months. Examined my priorities, backed off from work a little."

If only that were true, she thought. But true or not, it was a nice gesture on his part to devote that kind of time to her and Kyle. She reached out to brush her hand over his arm. "I didn't mean it that way, Matt. I meant that so many people depend on you. Some of their problems might not wait a week."

He squirmed in the seat. "It's not like I'll be completely out of touch. I'll only be a phone call away."

"Yes, but if you need to go back into town sooner, I want you to know I'll understand."

He scowled and stiffened. "I appreciate that."

"Because I know how important your work is...."

"Look." He shot her an angry glare. "I made a point of not scheduling anything pressing this week. It's not an inconvenience to get away for a few days."

"You made a point of..." She rubbed her palm up the cool skin of her arm. "Why?"

He let out an exasperated sigh and shook his head. "Because of the wedding."

"Matt, neither of us knew about our wedding until yesterday. You can't tell me..."

"Not *our* wedding," he barked. "*Your* wedding."

"My...?"

"To Roger Grant. Perhaps you recall the man?"

"Oh." She fell back against the seat and stared at the road stretching out before them. "I guess with all the hubbub I forgot about that fiasco for a minute. But why would my marriage affect your work schedule?"

Matt raked one hand through his hair and left a ruffled ridge in his wake. "I knew that the week after I had lost you for good, I'd be a little distracted—at the very least. I couldn't guarantee that I'd give my clients one hundred percent, so I planned to spend the week catching up on correspondence, rechecking files, cleaning the office, anything that kept me from dwelling on...things."

"I see." It was wrong, but Matt's disclosure made her feel almost giddy. Of course, she couldn't let him see that. She tapped her toe on the floorboard and tried to think of anything that might steer the conversation into safer waters.

Suddenly she heard Kyle in the back seat, babbling and clacking a set of oversize plastic keys together. She twisted around to speak to him. "Hey, there. You sure are in a better mood today."

"That's because his tooth finally poked through the gum last night."

"It did?" She started to lean over the seat to peek but Matt reprimanded her. She plunked back down and gave a hard yank to her shoulder belt to reposition it. "Well, darn it." She crossed her arms over her chest. "I wanted to see Kyle get his first tooth."

"I'm sure when Judge Harcourt put him in my care for the night, he never suspected something so auspicious would occur."

His grin baited her, but she didn't care. She thrust her lower lip out to better display her disappointment. "Well, I think it's just like two males—give them a boy's night out and they go and do something the female in their lives has been waiting to experience with them."

Matt snorted a laugh. "Are we talking about baby teeth or the time I went to that movie with a friend and you had a fit?"

"Not just any movie," she reminded him, the old ire rekindled.

Matt rolled his eyes. "For the millionth time, I'm sorry."

She laughed, then glanced over her shoulder and frowned. "Still, I really wished I'd been there when he cut his first tooth."

"Well, it only broke the surface enough to ease his discomfort. He didn't actually cut it yet."

She sighed.

"Tell you what," he said, swinging his arm out to place his hand on her knee. "We have all week. We'll just sit around and watch Kyle's tooth grow."

The image of the two of them sitting and staring intently into the baby's mouth assaulted Dani. She laughed. "Well, maybe we can think of a few other things to do this week."

Matt flexed his hand on her knee. Waves of heat, like those on a desert horizon, radiated from his hand and shimmered inside her. She swallowed hard and dropped her gaze to the source of her unsolicited pleasure. Matt's gaze fell to that spot as well.

He jerked his hand away but it hovered above her leg just long enough to create an awkward moment. He cleared his throat and replaced his hand on the steering wheel.

Dani bowed her head and picked at the patchwork of stamps on the corner of the large envelope in her lap.

"Whatcha got there?" Matt's voice seemed unnaturally cheerful.

"Oh—" Dani dived her hand into the packet "—Mom gave me these brochures of things to do at the bed and breakfast. I mean, around the bed and..."

She winced, hoping Matt would not think she'd been thinking about... *that*. Even if it had never been far from her thoughts ever since she realized she would finally be Matt's wife. She withdrew a handful of pamphlets and fanned them out for Matt's inspection. "See? Tourist information about the area close to Rosemont House."

"Sounds interesting." If he'd noticed her embarrassment, he kindly ignored it. "Maybe there's something we can do today."

"It is a beautiful day," she agreed wholeheartedly. "It would probably do Kyle a world of good to get out." And it would keep them from having to confront that great big bed lying in wait in their room.

"Okay, read off a few of the options," he said encouragingly.

She flipped open the first brochure. "There's an antique mall."

He shook his head.

"Um, a state historical park?"

He pretended to yawn.

"The Museum of Printers and Typesetters?"

His lip snarled up on one side and his brows slanted down over his questioning eyes.

"That's what it says." She waved the folded green paper at him.

"Anything else?"

"Here's a real possibility—a family farm and orchard."

"A farm?"

"You know, one of those pick-your-own fruit and vegetable places. Only this is an elaborate setup with a petting zoo, horseback riding, a craft store, a restaurant and a winery."

"A winery?" That perked him up. "Sounds like they have something for everybody. How far is it from Rosemont House?"

She noticed he didn't say "bed and breakfast." Somehow she doubted that mentioning a morning meal had him so cautious. She sighed and examined the pamphlet in her hand. "The farm is about ten miles south of Rosemont House. We can stop and unpack and be there in time for lunch."

"Great. That's our plan, then."

His staunch arms slackened a bit, confirming for Dani just how tense he'd been feeling. But tense about what? The makeshift marriage? Kyle's custody case? The week off from work? Or could he be feeling just as uptight about facing the inevitable as she was? She drummed her fingertips on the colorful stack of brochures in her lap and marveled at this turn of events.

Time and again she'd held Matt's libido at bay, choosing to wait to share his bed until they were married. Now they were legally husband and wife—and suddenly both of them would do anything to stay as far as possible from that beckoning bed.

* * *

"I don't know about you, but I can't wait to hit the sack." Matt held open the door for Dani.

She carried the half-asleep Kyle into their room in Rosemont House and immediately laid the baby down in his crib. "I really should give him a bath but I'm afraid it will only stir him up and we won't get him back to sleep."

Matt let the door fall shut and strode over to peer down at the infant. "I had no idea that one small person could get that messy in just a few hours."

"A few hours on a farm," she reminded him. She began to peel off the clothing sticking to his tiny body. "Did you see his face when you set him down in the straw?"

"He loved it." Matt laughed at the memory.

"So much he even ate some, I think." She dumped the dirty clothes on the floor. "He's amazing, isn't he?"

Matt bent down to pull a fresh diaper from the bag. He handed it to Dani. "I figured he'd start bawling when that goat nibbled on his shoe." He leaned over the crib to talk to Kyle. "But not this kid."

He put his hand on Kyle's rounded tummy and wriggled his fingers until the baby grinned. The sight penetrated Matt's heart. At last, he had his family. All that he had been striving for was his. An earnest release of good humor warmed his being. "No, Kyle wouldn't let an old goat scare him—not my boy."

Not *my* boy. The words fell between him and Dani like big blocks of ice. Her hands froze in the midst of the diapering. Matt wanted to say something, but what? He'd be damned if he'd retract the sentiment. As far as he was concerned, Kyle *was* his boy now—just as much as he was Dani's. That was a fact she would have to come to terms with one way or another.

"Um, you know what?" Dani lifted Kyle from his crib and held him close. "I think I will give him that bath."

She stood and started for the bathroom.

"Dani..."

"I don't need any help, thanks." She shut the door.

Matt followed, raising his fist to knock before just barging in. From inside the room, the gush of water filling the tub full force blotted out the sound of Dani fussing over Kyle. She'd shut him out—for now. But she couldn't keep that up indefinitely. Not with them sharing quarters this close. But what could he do to make her see how much he still cared? He'd married her. He'd gone to great lengths to help her keep the child she so dearly loved. He'd even come to love that child himself. What else remained that would convince her to give this relationship a real chance?

He turned on his heel and almost fell over the antique four-poster. Well, he thought, there's always that. He glanced over his shoulder at the door, scratched his jaw and shrugged. Why not? He threw himself across the massive bed, fixed a smile on his face and waited for Dani's return.

Chapter Six

Dani cupped her hand in the warm, soapy water and splashed a little on Kyle's chest. He clapped and gnashed his pink gums together in a smile.

"That's my baby," she cooed. *My* baby. Mine. Not Sarah or Veronica Delaney's. And not Matt's. She dabbed at Kyle's chin with a washcloth, hearing Matt's harmless remark replay in her mind.

My boy. He hadn't meant it as a threat. But she'd be foolish to ignore the significance of his possessive tone when he spoke of Kyle. Once he had helped her win custody from the Delaneys, would she have to fight Matt for those same rights? Oh, he wouldn't try to take Kyle from her legally—though thanks to their hasty marriage, he could certainly try.

She glanced down at the simple but elegant gold band on her left hand, marveling that just a short time ago Roger's ring had rested there. Now she and Matt shared a name and the responsibility toward a baby, if nothing else. What they had done today put them on equal footing to determine the course of Kyle's life. That was something she had counted on supervising by herself. But now?

What chance existed that after the case was settled, Matt would just walk away and have nothing more to do with the baby? None. None whatsoever. He was too honorable a man, one who did not take his obligations lightly, one who would choose to do the right thing over the easy thing. Dani sighed. Some of the very reasons she loved the man might well drive a wedge between them at some future date.

Kyle's head bobbed forward and startled her back to the present. "Poor baby, you're just too sleepy to enjoy your bath."

She rinsed him off and wrapped him in a big, fluffy bath towel. Now she had to go back out there and face Matt. She patted the baby and gave him a kiss on his warm, moist cheek for good measure. Then she swung the door inward with the most casual air she could muster.

"This is one pooped little trooper," she announced, breezing into the room.

"I have the formula mixed. Is he ready for a little night-cap?"

She heard Matt but made a point not to seek eye contact. Instead she made a beeline for Kyle's crib and laid the baby down. "I think he'll even skip the bottle tonight."

"You sure?"

"Yep. His main priority seems to be beddie-bye."

She straightened from over the crib and finally turned to face Matt. The sight of him stretched out across the turned-down bed in just his pajama bottoms stole the air from her lungs for a heartbeat. She lowered her head but her traitor-ous eyes remained glued to the tantalizing view. She coughed out a dry laugh. "I see Kyle's not the only one ready for bed."

Matt shrugged. Dani studied the width of his exposed shoulders. He sat up. She stared at the controlled ripple down his washboard stomach. He stood. She gawked at the hair defining the shape of his firm pecs. He swept his hand out to indicate the bed. Her hungry eyes filled with the vision of that body and that bed. She bit her lip and whimpered.

"It's been a heck of a day," Matt said, his arm still extended above the bed. "I think both you and I would benefit from a good..." He paused, as if searching for the right word, then a slow smile broke over his face.

Dani whipped around, snatched up Kyle's diaper and pajamas, then began dressing the drowsy infant.

"Night's rest." Matt moved in behind her as he concluded his provocative statement.

She took her time fitting Kyle into his fuzzy knit sleeper, ignoring Matt's nearness. Finally she finished and squeezed the snap at the collar shut. It popped like a firecracker in the prickling silence.

Dani straightened and found her spine pressed along Matt's abdomen. His body heat enveloped her. She tried to toss her hair back to show her cavalier attitude to his presence, but that only brought her profile in contact with his chest. His steady heartbeat thrummed against her own elevated pulse at her temple. She forced an airy tone through her tight vocal cords. "Well, I certainly could use some rest. So, since you took the floor the first night we spent here, I'll take my shift there tonight."

"Nope."

"I don't mind, Matt, really I don't. In fact, I insist."

"Uh-uh."

She tipped her head to glare at him. "Don't hand me any macho posturing."

"That's the last thing on my mind."

Dani gulped at the thought of the first thing on his mind. She rushed on with her argument to prevent either of them from dealing with that ticklish subject. "Please, Matt. You act like I'm the delicate female who must sleep in comfort. While you, the big strong male, requires little more than a rock for a pillow and a bearskin to keep the elements at bay while you sleep."

"Actually I never sleep in bare skin. Pajama bottoms are more my style," he teased.

"Yeah, I noticed." She crossed her arms over her chest. "But none of this changes my mind. I want you to take the bed tonight."

"I intended to all along." He shifted his bare feet to fit her into an increasingly intimate position.

"Then why'd you tell me no when I said I'd spend the night on the floor?"

"Because you're not sleeping on the floor."

She twisted her head around to narrow her eyes at him. Her mouth opened to reword the question, but he intervened.

"I'm not sleeping on the floor and you're not sleeping on the floor, because, Mrs. Taylor, we are both sleeping in that bed."

He cast a look over his shoulder, dragging Dani's own gaze reluctantly along. She swallowed. "But, Matt, I thought we agreed it wasn't going to be that kind of marriage."

"It's not." He bent his knees and without warning scooped Dani up into his arms. He smiled down at her with something barely contained and dangerous smoldering in his eyes. "At least not yet."

She laced her fingers behind his neck and laid her head under his chin. "Not yet?"

"Well, Dani, fate has dealt us some pretty strange twists these past few days. I don't want to tempt it by saying we'll never have *that kind of marriage*. Do you?"

Somehow she managed to shake her head and croak out, "No. No tempting. Tempting is bad."

Matt chuckled. "Well, not all bad."

"I meant . . ."

He pulled her closer. "I know what you meant. Now it's time for you to know what I mean."

He pivoted and headed with slow purpose toward the bed. "I've been a patient man about postponing our sex life, Dani."

A hard laugh leapt from her tight lips. "Is that what you call your behavior? Patient?"

He grinned at her. "Well, we dated almost two years and you're still . . . intact."

"Something you could've changed in a New York minute with one of these." She held her left hand aloft and wriggled her fingers. Her gold band flashed in the dim light.

Ever so gently, he laid her down on the soft bed, then straightened to gaze down at her. "Funny, all that time I tried to wrangle around your values and now that I've finally complied with them, I'm going to keep my hands off."

"You are?" She propped herself up on her elbows.

"I am." He pulled the covers up over her, then walked around to his side of the bed. "So, you see, there's simply no reason why we can't share this comfortable bed."

He sat down. She clutched at the side of the mattress to keep from rolling even slightly toward him.

Matt placed his right hand over his heart. He bent his head over her, making his hair tumble forward in a sweet disarray that called for Dani to smooth it down. She raised her hand. Matt caught it in midair, turned it and placed a kiss in her palm. She shuddered.

"You have my pledge not to try to seduce you," he whispered. "Do I have yours?"

She blinked, cocked her head, then nodded.

"Good." He sat up. "If we're going to rebuild our relationship, it has to be based on trust. This is as good a place to start as any."

"I agree." Her lips trembled but she managed to draw them into a smile.

"Then it's a deal." He shifted the position of her hand in his, giving it a vigorous shake.

She felt her forehead crinkle and let her expression speak for her.

Matt laughed, winked, then released her hand. He fell back against the headboard. "Ah, the traditional wedding night handshake." He turned his face to her. "Was it as good for you as it was for me?"

"You nut." She wadded the corner of her pillow in her fist and swung it around to hit him full in the chest. They both laughed. "Get some sleep."

"Yes, ma'am." He snapped off the lamp by his bedside.

She felt the bed shift as he settled into place. In the darkened silence Dani held her breath and waited. She dared not move until Matt had fallen into a deep sleep. Though she had been dead tired, the exchange with Matt had heightened her senses. She could feel his presence beside her, the warmth of his skin, the scent of his hair, the ragged rhythm of his breathing. All of it so close she need only roll onto her side to let her breasts brush against his arm. A wicked thrill crept over her. She shut her eyes, recalling the pledge they had made to wait.

Behind her eyes an earlier scene played in vivid color. She was sixteen. It was the eve of Matt's departure for college. They'd spent the evening doing the usual things—a movie, a burger, a drive that culminated at Rutger's Ridge, the local lover's lane. Even all these years later, she could feel his ips on hers, his eager hands on her skin. That night she'd let him slip his hand beneath her bra and thought herself deliciously brazen.

Matt had wanted to take the physical side of their relationship even further. Her body shivered anew at the memory of his words. *"I want to make you mine, Dani. Forever."*

Matt's. Forever. It still tempted her, but then, as now, she could not give him that. And he hadn't pushed her. That was the first time she'd realized just how much she'd loved him. The first time she'd known that beneath the macho facade of the town's star athlete was a boy striving for approval, for a sense of belonging that he'd never known, for love. Tears tingled along the sealed edges of her lids. How could she have been so wise so long ago? And where had that wisdom gone? When had she lost the ability to love the man beyond the drive and need to prove his worth to the outside world? Dani sighed and swiped away the tears that trickled down her temples.

She rolled her head to watch Matt sleeping, wondering if he ever thought of their life before their breakup. Did he ever dream of her?

Keep your eyes shut, your body still, your breathing calm and your lecherous longings in check. Matt repeated the list of commands for the tenth time since he'd shut the light off. He'd have gotten a hell of a lot better night's rest on the hard floor than he would ever get lying so close to Dani. But there was a method to his madness, he reminded himself.

Dani's love for him had grown cold. Yet, she hadn't completely shot him down when he'd suggested they try to repair their relationship. Maybe there was hope. As long as they had Kyle, he had time. He'd use that time to show her that he was still the man she had fallen in love with, that he could become the man she needed him to be.

*   *   *

The next few days passed much as that first, full of fun and making adventures for Kyle. The nights, on the other hand, got worse. If only he could work up some resentment toward Dani, or find some habit of hers truly annoying. Then he could focus on those instead of how sexy she looked in the morning with her hair mussed and her lips pouty. To further complicate matters, this time together had helped Matt rediscover the things he'd loved about Dani in the first place. Every time she teased him, or listened intently to him, or cuddled Kyle in her arms, he saw her inner joy, her genuine caring, the depths of her emotions. And it had almost driven him crazy.

He stood on the front porch of Rosemont House entranced by Dani and Kyle oohing and aahing over the swaying tulips along the sidewalk. He inhaled the scent of summer and smiled. Life was good. If Dani and Kyle really belonged to him, then life would be downright awesome. He stuffed his hands into the pockets of his slacks, thinking he could watch the two of them forever.

Unfortunately he couldn't even watch them for another few minutes. He waved to catch Dani's eye. She nodded and gave Kyle's little arm a jiggle to make it appear the baby had waved back. Kyle wrinkled his nose and snorted a laugh at the antics. The sight melted Matt's heart.

"So, you're finally off the phone," Dani said, strolling up the walkway to him. "We were beginning to think you'd forgotten our plans to go to that replica of an Amish community for dinner."

Matt shook his head. "We can't go anywhere for dinner, Dani."

"Why?" She clutched the baby higher on her hip. The suntanned glow on her face faded to ash. "Is something wrong? Something about the case?"

"That was Wayne Perry on the phone."

"The Delaneys' lawyer?" She came to the bottom of the steps and gazed up at Matt, her face filled with concern.

"Yes." Matt folded his arms over his chest. "I've known Wayne a long time. He called to keep me apprised of some new developments."

"Is that legal?" She moved up a step. "I mean, should you two be discussing the case, given the fact that you're adversaries?"

The corner of Matt's mouth lifted. "Neither of us betrayed our client's trust, if that's what you're asking. Besides, lawyers often negotiate points before it gets in front of a judge. Haven't you ever heard the term 'settling out of court'?"

She bolted up the rest of the stairs, stopping just as the toes of her tennis shoes touched his loafers. "Is that what happened, Matt? Did the Delaneys decide to settle out of court? Have they decided they don't want to fight for Kyle?"

"No, no." He grabbed her bare arms and anchored her in place. "Nothing like that, Dani. I was just giving an example."

Her thin shoulders slumped forward and she frowned. "Oh."

"No, Wayne called to relay some information—not all of it good."

"Not all, but some?" She tilted her head up. "Did he at least have some good news?"

The sunny tones had begun to return to her face. That, in turn, warmed Matt. He caressed the smooth skin of her firm upper arms. "Maybe good news is too optimistic. But it was interesting and I have a hunch, helpful."

"Really? What did he say?"

"It wasn't what he said as much as how he said it." He guided her over to the porch swing and waited until she and

Kyle were situated before settling in himself. "Sarah an
Veronica are already getting on their lawyer's nerves."

"What a surprise." Dani rolled her eyes.

"Yeah, well, his frustration led him to show a little mor
of his hand than he probably intended." He planted his fe
on the wooden floor, bracing his long legs out, then bend
ing his knees to set the swing in a pleasing rhythm. "I got th
impression from Wayne that the ladies would be content t
let this custody case drag on indefinitely."

"So that they wouldn't have to actually take care o
Kyle?"

"That's about the size of it." He scratched the baby
bulging belly with one finger.

Dani dangled her bare legs, letting them bounce agains
the edge of the swaying seat. "That's good news for us, isn
it? The longer we have Kyle, the better our case."

Matt gripped the armrest until the roughened woo
scraped his palm. "That might be best for our case, bu
what about us? What about Kyle?"

Her brow pleated down over her clear green eyes. "I don
understand."

"The best thing for Kyle is to have a home. To have sta
bility."

"We can give him that." She thrust out her lower lip.

"But we'll be in legal limbo. We won't be able to d
something as simple as take an out-of-state vacation with
out the court's permission."

"Really?"

He nodded. "I've seen this kind of thing in divorce cases
You may live at the mercy of the Delaneys. If they don't lik
something you're doing with Kyle they can take you to cour
and ask the judge to stop you—or threaten to pick up th
fight to take him away."

"I never thought of that." She pulled Kyle into her la
and locked her hands around his middle.

"You also probably didn't think of this..." He halted the wing in motion and lowered his face to within inches of ers. "As long as there's an ongoing court case, we'll have o stay married."

Her eyes sparked with emotion, which Matt struggled to define. Though he didn't dare let his heart hope, his mind old him that if she had spoken in that moment, she might have confessed it never occurred to her *not* to stay married o him.

Dani focused her attention on the baby. "So, is that the ad news or the...helpful news?"

"Helpful—at least in as much as it gives me an idea about ow to handle the Delaneys."

She puffed out a hard breath. "Gee, I don't know if I can stand hearing the bad news."

"I'll warn you, it isn't pretty." He leaned back and squinted out into the sun-washed front yard. "It involves our ex-fiancé."

"Roger?"

"Yeah, Roger." Matt stretched his arm out behind Dani. 'Seems he's had a busy few days."

Dani pulled Kyle closer, like a child clinging to a teddy bear. Her voice conveyed her dread as she said, "What's he been up to?"

Matt clenched his fist. "For starters, he's been pressuring Wayne to rush the custody case—and to go for blood."

"No." She gasped and dragged Kyle closer still. The baby kicked and squirmed in protest.

Matt very gently pulled Kyle free and placed him in the nook between their two bodies. "Yes. Wayne told me about Roger's meddling because he'd hoped you could persuade him to back down before things got nasty. Unfortunately it may already be too late for that."

She laid her hand on Matt's thigh. "What has he done?"

"Seems good old Roger has been going around tow spreading ugly rumors."

"What could Roger possibly say?" Her fingers curle into the flesh of his tensed leg and Matt had to stave off th wave of desire it shot through him.

He gingerly removed her hand and cradled it in his "Honey, he's running his mouth off all over town about us He's saying, well, that we don't have a real marriage— therefore our home is not the most stable environment fo the baby."

"But Judge Harcourt recommended—no, he practicall forced us to get married because it *would* be best for Kyle."

"Apparently Roger found a way to smear us withou making the judge look bad." Matt hung his head for a mo ment to escape the abject fear and confusion in Dani's eyes "Roger is saying we let the judge believe that because of ou past involvement, we were willing to make a real and last ing marriage when that wasn't our intention at all."

"As for lasting marriage, nobody gets a guarantee of on of those these days." She raised her chin in defiance. "An as for the other...well, what does he mean by that any way? A real marriage?"

He placed his forehead to hers. "What do you think h means?"

She jerked her head away so that he found his nose bur ied in the sweet perfume of her brunette curls. "There' more to a real marriage than sex."

Matt inhaled until his lungs ached. "I'm sure that's true but..."

"And where does Roger Grant get off passing judgmen on what constitutes a valid marriage?" She pushed up fron the swing, pivoted to face him and crossed her arms unde her breasts.

Matt stared at her and shrugged. Dani shook her hea and began to pace the short distance from the porch rail t the house and back. "Roger never loved me and I never loved him. Some people might have questioned the authenticity of that type of marriage. And they'd certainly have cause to question our intentions, or wonder how long our commitment might last."

Matt leaned forward, using one hand to brace the baby in place at his side.

The intensity of his gaze followed Dani, but she refused to let it daunt her. "Regardless of our feelings for each other, if I'd have married Roger it would have been real." She spun and nailed him with a warning glare. "And I don't mean because we'd have had sex."

He raised an eyebrow but kept his lips sealed.

"A common bond." She pointed one finger at him. "That would have made our marriage real. Roger and I shared similar goals and wanted the same things from life. That's what we would have made a commitment to—to helping each other realize our individual dreams."

"And you would have settled for that?" He picked up the baby and stood. "Dani, I don't think I can believe what I'm hearing."

"Why?" She pressed her palms to the porch rail. The freshly painted wood squawked under the weight of her straight-armed stance. "People marry for all sorts of reasons, Matt. Some for companionship, others because of family pressures, unexpected pregnancies, financial considerations..."

"And love?"

She stiffened. "Of course, love."

"But that wasn't the case with you and Roger?" He hoisted Kyle up to rest in the crook of his arm. "You honestly didn't love the man, not even a little?"

"I... I respected him."

Matt choked out a bitter laugh.

"Respected," she said emphatically. "Past tense. Now..."

"Now?"

"Now, I'd like to ring his scrawny neck." She circled her hands around the rail, gripping it until her knuckles shone white. "Boy, I'd give anything to go back to Woodbridge and show him up for the meanspirited, self-absorbed creep that he is."

Matt slapped his hand to his thigh. "Yes."

Dani's grip faltered at the sound and a spray of tiny splinters gouged her hand. Luckily none penetrated too deeply and she quickly brushed them away. When her heart had resettled in her chest, she threw her shoulders back and half sat on the railing. "Yes? Yes what?"

"Yes, we'll go back to Woodbridge and do exactly what you suggested."

"What I suggested?"

"We'll demonstrate to old Roger—and the rest of the town—that we have a viable relationship." He bowed his head to plant a kiss on the baby's head. "That Kyle is better off with us in any arrangement than with the Delaneys."

If not for that spontaneous gesture, she might have told him to forget it. Even without knowing exactly what Matt had in mind, the thought of parading her private life in front of her small town made her cringe. "Just how do you propose we put on this demonstration?"

"We set up housekeeping." Matt grinned at her.

To say her knees went weak would be a vast understatement. Her whole body went liquid. Housekeeping. With Matt Taylor. How many years had she dreamt of it?

"Don't look so shocked, Dani," he teased. "We are married. What did you think we would do when we went back home anyway?"

She swallowed and shook her head.

He brought the baby to her. "So, we go back to town and you move into my house. We establish a routine, let people get used to seeing us as husband and wife and as Kyle's parents. That, coupled with a few choice words to Grant should turn the tide in our favor."

She curled Kyle closer and blinked up at Matt. "Well, I suppose it wouldn't hurt to try."

"Good. Let's go pack. The sooner we get this under way, the sooner we'll stop the town gossip." He moved to the front door and held it open for her.

Dani wandered inside the house half dazed as she heard Matt say, "And the sooner you confront Grant, the better."

That chance came sooner than Dani could have dreamt. Later that evening, after they had gotten settled in Matt's house, she had volunteered to run to the grocery store to pick up a few things. As she hurried outside the store with her purchases, a familiar figure approached.

Roger spotted her immediately. She waved him over. His lanky body seemed more angular than usual in his navy suit. Her gaze traveled to his face and to the new, severe haircut that made his nose appear more hawkish than ever. What had she ever found attractive about this man? He gave her a chilly smile made eerie by his empty eyes.

Suddenly she recalled why she had been drawn to Roger. It was the fact that she found him utterly unattractive. She had wanted a man who would never inspire passion, jealousy, love, hatred, or any strong emotion in her. She'd wanted the exact opposite of Matt. And she'd found it.

"Well, hello, *Mrs. Taylor.*" Roger sneered.

"Hello, Roger." She popped open her car trunk, then glanced around the small parking lot. Not only were they alone, but the dim evening light would make them hard to see by any passersby. Perfect. She plunked the plastic grocery sacks into the car, then turned to him. "I was hoping you could spare me a few minutes to talk."

He stuffed his hands into his pockets. "Oh? Aren't you worried about making your *husband* jealous?"

Dani slammed the trunk shut. When she moved closer to him, she gritted her teeth in an achingly pleasant smile. "Roger," she said with feigned sweetness, "I've heard something recently that I just can't believe."

"What's that, Dani? Your wedding vows?"

She'd kill him—with kindness, of course. She opened her purse and rummaged for a moment, then produced the engagement ring he had given her. Holding it out to him, she said, "First, let me return this. Then, let me ask if you're spreading unkind stories about Matt and me."

Roger glared down at the ring. He snatched it away from her roughly. "All I've done is tell a few people the truth. If it's unkind or unflattering, that isn't my fault."

"Oh, Roger, don't be that way." She batted her lashes at him, knowing it would have no effect. "It's not like you lost the great love of your life."

"No." He jammed the ring into his pocket. "I lost something more precious—my future." He pushed up his glasses with one bent knuckle. "You and I made plans, Dani. Your actions have cost me the life I assumed I'd be living right now."

"Life doesn't always abide by our plans, Roger."

"No, but this time it was you who didn't abide by the plan." He huffed out an angry sigh.

"And so you want to punish me by trying to hurt my chances of adopting Kyle?"

''I want you to come to your senses. I want you to admit that your marriage to Taylor is a fraud. I want to know that even if I can't have you, neither can he.''

Dani swallowed and tried to think out the implications of such an admission. But all she could think was that this was her opportunity to make Roger back off of the custody case. ''And if I said you were right, Roger, what would it change? You'd still wage this smear campaign, trying to prevent my adopting Kyle.''

''Not necessarily.'' He crossed his long arms over his narrow chest.

''What are you saying? You'd stop working against me?'' Her heart raced. ''Why? What would be in it for you?''

''A date. With you.'' He smirked. ''When this charade of a marriage is over, I want you to promise you'll go out with me. You do that and I'll back down.''

An icy heaviness filled Dani's stomach. Masculine pride could be a very ugly thing, she decided. ''You're not interested in me at all. Matt humiliated you by marrying your bride right out from under you. What you want is revenge.''

''A date with Taylor's ex-wife would certainly give me the last laugh,'' he snickered.

''And in exchange, you'd keep your mouth shut about the case?''

''Well, that would be in my best interest, too, wouldn't it?'' He stepped close to whisper, ''Not much glory in dating a man's ex-wife if everyone thought it was a phony marriage.''

Roger was making it too easy for her. The promise of a date *if* she and Matt ever divorced. It wasn't even a lie. But could she trust him? She stared into his eyes. What choice did she have? ''Okay, Roger, you've got a deal.''

Her handshake was quick and clean just like her getaway. On the ride home she sang along with the radio at the top of her lungs. She told herself it was the excitement of besting Roger that made her do it. But deep down she knew, she was just trying to drown out that tiny voice inside her head that kept saying, "You've just made a bargain with the devil and this time even Matt might not be able to get you out."

Chapter Seven

"Matt?" Dani jostled Kyle on her hip and called up the stairs. "Your breakfast is—"

Matt approached her from behind, barreling down the hallway that connected the kitchen to the foyer. He brushed past her with a piece of toast hanging from between his teeth.

"—ready." She finished her sentence. "I thought you were still getting dressed."

"I am." He slid his black suit jacket up onto his shoulders. He pulled the toast away from his mouth to plant a sparse kiss on her cheek then Kyle's head. "Gotta go."

"But, Matt, I need to talk to you," she protested with a stamp of her shoe.

Matt glanced at his wristwatch. He had big plans brewing—plans that just might make the difference between a happy marriage and an unavoidable divorce. He didn't have time to stand around gabbing. "Later this afternoon you'll have my undivided attention. Right now, I have some very important phone calls to make. After that, I'll grab the things I need to work on our case and head home."

Matt tore off a shred of the toast. He popped the buttery bread into his mouth and forced it down with a hard swallow. "I'll be back by noon and you'll have me underfoot all week."

"Why do I feel like if I let you out that front door I'll lose you to one work-related crisis after another?" She scowled.

"You have my word, Mrs. Taylor. For this entire week, I will devote all my energy to you and Kyle." He lifted his briefcase from the foyer floor.

Dani gritted her teeth. She didn't have to say what was on her mind. The play of emotions in her eyes told him everything.

"I know, I've broken promises like that before..."

"Broken them? You've demolished them. Do you have any idea how many weekends I've had to cancel plans, waiting for you to do 'one more thing' at the office?"

"I know." He shook his head at his own foolhardiness. For an instant, he thought about confessing his scheme to prevent that from happening in the future. But one look at her hardened gaze changed his mind. She didn't trust him to do something as simple as come home for lunch. How could she believe him when he told her he had an idea that would literally cut his workload in half without jeopardizing the practice he'd labored so long to build? No, this was something he'd have to show her.

He smiled and patted her shoulder. "I've been a jerk. But that's changed and I'll prove it to you—starting today, when I keep my word and come home at noon."

He chomped down another bit of the crumbling toast and turned on his heel.

"Hold it right there, buster," she bellowed. Kyle startled in her arms. Matt jerked his shoulders back. "What I need to talk to you about is important, won't take long and needs your immediate attention. I shouldn't have to wait until noon to find out if you've really changed.''

Busted. He let his briefcase fall to the tile floor with a thud. "Okay, I can spare a few minutes."

She hoisted Kyle higher on her hip, hiking up the hem of her oversize T-shirt. "Do you realize that in two weeks I go back to work at the hospital?"

She shook off his attempt to comment with a toss of her dark curls. "I'm interviewing baby-sitters today and I hoped to have your input."

"Input?" He blinked at her and swallowed down the last bite of toast. "You're right, that won't take long to address."

"Oh?"

"Absolutely."

"Then, what's your recommendation? A day-care center? A home-based care-giver? A nanny?"

"No. No. And no." He drew Kyle from her arms and screwed his face into an amusing expression for the child's enjoyment. Kyle opened his mouth in a silent laugh. "My recommendation," Matt said, "is that you don't hire anyone at all."

"Then who'll take care of Kyle?" She arched her eyebrows at him and planted her hands on her hips.

Matt arched his eyebrows right back at her. He didn't say a word but he telegraphed his meaning loud and clear.

"Me?" She thumped her chest. "I wouldn't need to hire a baby-sitter if I were available to take care of him myself."

"See?" He extended one arm, his palm turned upward. "Problem solved."

"Matt..."

"Gotta go." He leaned in to pass her the baby.

Dani refused to meet him halfway. "You're not being fair. You expect me to completely alter everything about my life to suit you. But I don't see you making any changes in your life-style to accommodate our new status."

"That's not true, Dani," he said softly, mischief jouncing merrily through his entire body.

She cocked her head.

"I've made one very radical change." He leaned over her so that she could not avoid his teasing gaze. "Since we've been married, I've completely given up sex."

Flame rose in her cheeks. She swung her arm to point to the door. "Out."

"It was a joke, Dani." He chuckled and pinched the tip of her nose.

She reached out to take Kyle and muttered, "I just thought we needed to talk, that's all."

"You're right." He closed in on her and the baby. "And when I get home this afternoon, we'll talk."

She pushed her lower lip out, determined to show her discontent.

"Aw, don't be like that. I will be home around noon, I swear."

"Yeah, after hearing that flimsy promise for the millionth time, I'm ready to swear, too."

Matt groaned. "Okay, here's the deal—we'll make a date of it."

She threw him an interested but skeptical glance.

"Not only will I be back here by noon, I'll bring lunch with me. What do you say?"

"I say, it's a great idea, but pardon my cynicism if I keep a sandwich in the fridge just in case my lunch date is late—or fails to show at all." She jiggled Kyle on her hip.

"You won't need it, I promise. Now, I've got to go." He leaned down to give her a quick kiss, then turned to leave.

In her arms, Kyle squealed with anger so real, his entire body trembled. He thrust out his hands, his fat little fingers straining uncontrolled just to reach Matt's arms.

"No, Kyle." Matt placed a kiss on the pink tips of the child's splayed fingers. "I can't stay. I have to go to work."

Dani took Kyle's hands in hers and spoke in a soothing voice. "It's okay, sweetie, Daddy says he'll be back soon."

"Daddy?" Matt cocked his head. Glare from the morning sun reflected in the foyer and blotted out Dani's expression. He had no way of knowing if she felt chagrin at the slip of the tongue or if she'd intended to call him Kyle's father. He couldn't walk away on that uncertain note. He stepped closer to her. His voice gruff with emotion, he whispered, "Do you realize that's the first time you've called me 'Daddy' in front of Kyle?"

He bent his head. The light from the window at his back cast a golden halo glow over her sweet face. She nodded.

Humbled. No other term would quite describe Matt's emotion then. His mouth twitched. He wanted to say something but simply couldn't find the words.

Dani looked up into his face. She smiled ever so softly.

Matt moved back to her. He lowered his head, his lips forming a silent thank-you as they closed over hers. He pressed as close as he dared with the baby between them. Flashes of sensation bolted through his body. In that kiss he communicated the strain of holding back his love for so long.

Dani responded in kind. She dug the fingers of one hand into his shoulders and moaned.

Just then, Kyle squirmed and fussed.

Matt pulled away. His gaze melded with hers and they stood in tableau for what seemed minutes. Then, Dani smiled, punched Matt lightly in the arm and said, "Go on and get out of here, you big lug. We both have a lot of work to do before lunch."

"See you later." Matt hurried out.

Once the door had shut, the baby quieted. He laid his head on her shoulder. His body shuddered twice. Then he sighed.

"Everything is going to work out fine, sweetheart." She patted Kyle's back as she ascended the stairs. A tiny twinge of guilt stabbed her conscience to see how attached Kyle had become to Matt. She wondered if, in the final analysis, this sham marriage might have very bad consequences for the child. The memory of Matt's kiss assaulted her. And for her.

She walked into the spare bedroom where she had placed her things after they returned to Woodbridge. Matt's house had four bedrooms—a huge master and three smaller ones. He made no pretense of the fact that he had the place built for the family he had hoped to have with her. Everyone in town knew it. But she had never even seen the entire house until she moved in.

She spun around to stare into the master bedroom directly across the hall. Matt's wayward comment about giving up sex reverberated in her head. How many other women had seen this house before her? Had any slept alongside Matt in his big, Western pine bed?

A strange amalgam of emotion jangled in her stomach. She bit her lip and took a step toward Matt's room. Suddenly Kyle cried to get down. The spell shattered. She blinked at the baby, then sat him down on the thick blue carpet. As she straightened she noticed the red pin-striped wallpaper and could almost see baseball pennants and sports posters hanging there. "If we were going to stay permanently, this would probably be your room, slugger."

Kyle gurgled and reached for one of Dani's navy pumps lying on the floor beside the bed. He immediately popped the toe of the shoe into his mouth.

"No, no." She took the shoe away. Kyle grinned up at her, drool bathing his chubby chin. She laughed. "I need to wear this shoe today when I interview care-givers."

Kyle flopped onto his belly and stretched out to grasp Dani's other shoe. She got there first and scooped up the endangered pump. She shook the shoe in Kyle's direction and admonished, "You're a sneaky one, aren't you?"

He rolled onto his back and gave her his charming noiseless laugh. She caved in. In one step she stood over him, then sank to her knees. "Oh, Kyle, what am I supposed to do?"

He kicked his legs in the air. She gently pinched his toes. "I want to do what is best for you, but how? I have to work to provide for you and to give you a good role model. Not that I wouldn't be a good role model staying home."

Kyle slapped one chubby hand on his leg and let out a happy yelp.

"Yes, I know, Matt would be glad to provide for both of us, but is that all he's capable of? We need someone who will be there for us, and not just as a breadwinner."

The baby cooed.

"Okay, so I admit he's more than just a breadwinner, he's also one heck of a good kisser." She pressed the back of her hand to her still-tingling lips and sighed. "You know, Kyle, right now I have everything I ever dreamed I wanted. A home, a baby, a husband, a career. And yet, I'm so confused."

She pulled the child into her lap and smoothed her palm over his wispy hair. "Of course, in my dreams, I had time to get things in proper order. First, I'd have the husband and time to adjust to married life. Next, I'd have nine months to prepare for a baby, then I'd be ready to address the whole working mother issue. Let that be a lesson to you." She pulled him away from her chest, turned him to face her and rubbed his little nub of a nose with hers. "Life doesn't always go as planned. At least not my life. Your daddy's life, however, seems to always be on an even keel—practically presenting him with whatever he wants."

She began dressing the baby without paying attention to the task. "No, Matt really does have it all. The home, the family, even me, without having to abandon his first love—his career."

She picked Kyle up and glared into his innocent blue eyes. "You can bet your pacifier that he won't show up for our lunch date. Or, if he does, I will not have, as he put it, his undivided attention."

She spun around and caught a glimpse of herself in the dresser mirror. She cringed. Her baggy outfit was hardly deserving of any man's attention. That's when an idea hit her. An idea so devious, so delicious, so dangerous she dared not try it. Or did she?

Dani spent the rest of the morning meeting with prospective care-givers. By eleven o'clock she had narrowed the possibilities down to four. By eleven-fifteen she had handed Kyle off to her mother. At ten till twelve she stood in front of her dresser mirror and assessed her image.

"I can't." She tugged at the lace edging on the white silk bustier she'd purchased months ago when her marriage to Matt had seemed imminent. The satin ribbon refused to budge. She gulped down as much air as the garment allowed and switched her tactic. Her fingers fumbled to free the sheer stocking from the lacy garter at her thigh. It stretched slightly but would not come undone.

"Hi, honey, I'm home." Matt's voice boomed through the entire house, shaking the very walls.

No, wait. The only thing shaking was her. What had she been thinking when she'd wriggled her way into this slinky getup?

"Dani? Are you home? I brought lunch."

"I'll be right there, Matt." She had to think the way she looked—fast. Nothing she owned would conceal this outfit properly. She needed something oversize. Her gaze fell on one of Matt's shirts that she'd offered to mend. In a flurry of movement, she threw it on with the wraparound skirt she'd worn earlier that morning.

"I'll meet you in the kitchen," she called out as she descended the stairs, rolling up her long sleeves, and tucking in the shirttail as she went. When her stiletto heels hit the hard foyer floor, she stopped to remove them.

"Dani?" Matt's tone had grown impatient. "Where are you?"

"On my way." No time to take off the shoes, she needed every second of the walk down the hall to button the shirt. She reached for a button. Nothing. Her pace slowed. She moved her fingers upward. Again nothing. That's when she remembered her offer to sew all new buttons on the shirt. She groaned through her clenched teeth.

"Dani? Come and get it while it's still hot."

"Maybe that should be my line," Dani muttered as she glanced down at her exposed bustline. Quickly she crossed one side of the shirt over the other and tightened her wrapped skirt to hold it in place. That would have to do. With as much grace as the situation allowed, she entered the sunny kitchen.

"Well, hello, stranger," she said, hoping the lightness in her words would cover for being out of breath.

"What took so long? Your pizza is getting cold." Matt stood to pull out one of the ladder-back chairs at the gleaming pine kitchen table.

"Pizza?" Dani squinted suspiciously at the big flat white box as she settled into her seat.

Matt leaned down, putting his mouth next to her ear.

She clutched the shirt to keep it from gaping open.

"I've got something here that'll thrill you to your toes."

"Isn't that a coincidence?" She laughed nervously, imagining how Matt might react to her own little surprise. "What is it?"

"Only your very favorite."

"Not?" She turned so quickly the tip of her nose brushed his cheek. She bit her lip to keep from nuzzling him.

"Voilà! Ham, mushroom and pineapple." He flipped open the pizza box with a flourish.

The rich aroma of the steaming pizza drew her reluctantly away from Matt. She placed both hands on the table and shut her eyes to make a show of inhaling the mingled scent of smoky meat, spicy sauce and sweet fruit.

Matt moved around to seat himself across from her. He dipped into the box to work free one large slice. "Here you go." He plopped the piece down on a napkin in front of her. "So, is Kyle asleep?"

Suddenly self-conscious about arranging to be alone with him, Dani ducked her head. "Um, no. Mom has him. She, um, wanted to spend some time with him."

"Then we're alone?" His soft, precarious tone thrummed down Dani's spine.

She shimmied in her seat. A garter snap bit into the tender flesh at the back of her thigh. She stilled physically but her mind raced on to find some way to distract Matt—and herself. She found it in the stack of résumés resting nearby. "Um, yes, we're alone. That gives us the perfect chance to discuss these."

Matt frowned at the papers.

She tapped on the top page. "These are the best résumés from the women I interviewed today. Why don't you check them out and tell me what you think."

He angled his dubious gaze at her from the corner of his eyes. Then he focused in on the top paper.

Dani bunched together the overlapping front of her borrowed shirt and waited. Matt's dark brows clashed in stern consideration. She leaned forward, hoping to prompt him to say something.

"No." He picked up the page and with a flick of his wrist sent it swirling to the floor.

Dani jumped. She tried to speak but never got the chance. "No." He sent the next résumé sailing.

She tried to catch the paper as it rustled past her knee, but it slipped away. "Matt..."

"No." The third résumé somersaulted down to land beside the others on the honey-colored hardwood floor.

He took more time with the last one. He moved his gaze down the length of the page once. Twice. He lifted his eyes to hers. She caught her breath.

"Never." He slammed his splayed hand on the paper. He crunched the paper into a crumpled ball and dropped it into the résumé graveyard he'd created at their feet.

She glowered at him and gathered up the forsaken résumés. Matt watched her press the worst creases out of the crumpled one. "How could you think I'd find any of these people an acceptable substitute for you? Kyle deserves the best, Dani, and that's you."

"It's not as though I'm talking about deserting him, Matt. Just putting him in someone else's care for a few hours a day."

"So you can go and attend to some other kid's needs?"

"That's a low blow and totally uncalled for."

True. But Matt didn't have the luxury of lengthy debates; he had to make Dani see things his way, now. Because if Dani went back to work, she'd eventually be able to support Kyle by herself. Then why would she need him? He wanted her to need him—even if it was only to help her make a better life for Kyle. But he couldn't tell her that. Could he? He jerked his head up. "Dani..."

"Don't." She held her hand up. "Spare me your outdated, male chauvinistic attitudes about working women." She stood. The sudden action tipped her chair up on its back legs. It teetered there a moment, then crashed to the floor.

Matt pushed his own seat back in surprise but Dani didn't miss a beat; she went on with her anger-fueled speech.

"If I would choose to stay home with the baby it would be because that's what is best for *all* of us, not just what's easiest for you, Matt Taylor."

"Dani, I wasn't..."

She threw her arms out to her sides and rolled her eyes heavenward. "And to think, I was all ready to greet you in this."

She yanked at the ties of her waistband. The skirt plummeted with a soft whisking sound to the ground around her high heels. The huge shirt she had folded over her body fell open.

"What the..." Matt felt his jaw slacken and he wondered if his eyes were literally bulging out of his head. He ogled Dani's lovely body in virginal white lingerie that suggested anything but purity. His heart thundered. He struggled to say something suave and romantic but all the blood that nourished the thinking part of his brain had gone elsewhere. He shifted in his suddenly too restrictive trousers and let out a low whistle. "Man, oh, man."

"Man? Guess again." Dani laughed. "If I were a man, I don't think you'd have that dog-in-the-butcher-shop expression on your face, Matt."

"Huh?" Oh, that was real smooth. He cleared his throat and shook his head. His gaze swept over her, appreciating every nuance from the sexy shoes to the blush on her high, round breasts. "I guess you can tell you've caught me completely off guard." He closed in on her. "Not that I mind."

"Hold it right there, Matt." Dani held her hand up. She bent at the knees to scoop up the clothes she had discarded. "I only put this stuff on because I wanted to get your attention."

"You've got it." He stepped even closer. "Now, what do you plan to do with it?"

She held the bundled shirt and skirt between them. "I..." She swallowed hard. "I honestly didn't think that far ahead."

He placed his hands on her smooth shoulders. "Then, perhaps you'll allow me to make a few suggestions."

She bit her lip and gazed up at him. He clenched his jaw and waited, inhaling the sweet scent of her warm body so close to his. She wanted to say yes. He could feel it.

"Matt, I..."

"Yes?"

She wet her lips, then parted them to speak again.

A sudden, shrill ringing pierced the weighty silence. Dani turned toward the kitchen telephone.

"Let it ring," Matt barked.

"I can't. What if something's wrong with Kyle?"

He released her. The moment had passed. She rushed to the phone and had herself covered with his shirt before she picked up the receiver.

"Hello?"

Matt turned his back to her, willing the burning below his belt line to quell. Dani's voice became a muffled background sound to his own thoughts. Would she have given in to him? And if she did, what then? The image of her in that lingerie seized his senses. After the obvious, of course. Giving him her body was not the same as giving him her heart. With any other woman on earth, he'd have welcomed the separation. But with Dani, he wanted the whole package.

"Matt?"

He pivoted to face her again.

She held the receiver out to him. "It's Wayne Perry for you."

In two long strides he was at her side. "Hey, Perry, what's up?"

Matt tried to concentrate on what Wayne had to say, but with Dani dressing just a few feet away from him, it was not an easy thing to do. Finally he got the gist of the other man's message. "No can do, pal."

"No can do what?" Dani's brows slanted down over her eyes in concern.

Matt covered the mouthpiece. "Wayne wants to play a round of golf with me."

"Golf?"

Matt shrugged. "Not all business gets done over a desk, Dani."

"Business?" She jolted to attention. "As in the custody case?"

Matt scowled. "He won't say for sure. He could have some kind of settlement to propose or he may just want to spend the afternoon on the links."

"Well, I think you should go and find out."

"Are you sure? It will mean I'll be late for dinner."

"That's fine. I don't mind if it's for a good cause." She patted his back. "Maybe I'll make use of the time to get some more things from Mom's. And if you get home before I do, you can just heat up the leftover pizza."

Matt sighed and removed his hand from the mouthpiece. "Okay, Perry. Looks like the little woman can live without me for a few hours. Meet you there in twenty minutes."

"Here." Dani shoved a slice of pizza at him. "Better eat on the way to the golf course."

Matt accepted the cold slab. Dani gave his shoulders a quick squeeze as she chattered on enthusiastically. "Gosh, I hope Wayne has some good news. Wouldn't that just make your day?" She released him and rushed out of the room.

Matt stared at the limp triangle of pizza smothered in co-agulated cheese. He bit down and tore off the pointed tip.

"Guess it's only fitting," he muttered as he chewed and swallowed. "First she gives me the cold shoulder, then a cold lunch. What next?'' He took another bite and answered his own question with his mouth full. ''What's next? The way this day is going, I have no doubt that I'll end it by taking a nice, long, cold shower.''

Chapter Eight

Matt stepped into the blasting shower spray. The warm water flooded over his tired muscles and helped him relax. What a day. First, anxiety over losing Dani to self-sufficiency made him act like a jerk. Then the whole lingerie fiasco.

He laid his head back against the slick gray tiles of the shower stall and shut his eyes—as if that could block out the vision of untouchable Dani in silk and lace. He sighed out a curse, then straightened.

To top the whole day off, he'd played bad golf for four hours just to get thirty seconds worth of information. He snapped off the water and dried his body quickly, wrapping one towel around his waist and draping another over his head. He lumbered into the bedroom, rubbing his hair dry as he went.

Right now all he wanted was a cool drink, something mindless on TV and a good night's rest. His gaze fell on the big, inviting bed. Well, that wasn't *all* he wanted. But that was all he was going to get.

He slipped into a pair of gym shorts and a T-shirt and started into the upstairs hallway.

"Look, Kyle, I told you Daddy would be here to tuck you in tonight," Dani said from the stairway.

The instant Kyle saw Matt, he screeched with delight. At least, Matt thought it was delight. He stopped and waited for Dani to bring the child to him.

"Nice of you to finally get home." The sarcasm stung his own ears even as the words left his mouth. But he couldn't help it. Pangs of sexual frustration mixed with the fear that someday Dani and Kyle would not return to his home, had left Matt edgy.

Dani stilled at the top of the stairs. "Do you have bad news or are you just a grouch on principle?"

Matt shrugged a passable apology and reached out to take the baby. "What's this I hear about someone needing to be tucked in?"

Kyle poked two fingers into his mouth and snuggled under Matt's chin. "What did this kid do all day to get so worn-out?"

"I'll tell you later," Dani said, pointing him in the direction of Kyle's crib. "First, I want to hear your news."

"Nothing much to tell, really. Wayne just used me as something of a sounding board.

Dani moved ahead of him into the room. Inside, she flicked on the soft, moon-shaped night-light on the dresser.

Matt carried the baby into the dimly lit room and laid him gently inside the crib. "Apparently the cousins have missed their last two appointments with Wayne."

"And?"

Matt offered the pacifier to the baby, who latched onto it like a lifeline. "Are you sure he's not hungry?"

"He just spent the day at my mother's." Impatience colored Dani's words. "Do you think she'd send him home hungry?"

"Guess not," Matt said. He patted the baby, then backed away.

Kyle curled into a ball with the toe of his pale blue sleeper grasped in one hand. When he noticed their faces, he worked the rubber pacifier into his mouth a little faster. He peeked between the white crib rails, his blue eyes bleary with drowsiness.

"What about changing him?" Matt asked.

Dani let out a furious groan and charged up to him, then grabbed the front of his T-shirt in her hand. "Tell me about the cousins," she demanded.

Matt placed one raised finger to his lips to quiet her, then undid her knotted fingers from his shirt. "Wayne says he has another appointment set up in two days. If they don't show for that..."

"We get to keep Kyle?" Her hushed tone did not conceal the depths of her excitement.

At the mention of his name, the baby roused. He labored at lifting his head, gnawing furiously on the pacifier all the time. Dani held her breath. Kyle succumbed. His head dropped to the smooth cotton sheet but he continued to watch them.

Matt smiled wistfully at the infant. "I wish I could say for sure that we're going to keep him. All I'm prepared to say now is that the Delaneys' behavior won't show favorably. They haven't given Wayne much to work with and with the hearing less than a week away, it's not likely that they will."

She smoothed one hand down his arm. "Thanks."

"If anyone can take credit for it, it's you." He flattened his palm on her back, savoring the feeling of the thick curls tickling his fingers. "Whatever you said to Grant must have worked. He's really backed down."

Dani glanced down and shuffled her feet. The memory of her talk with Roger weighed like a stone on her conscience. Her bargain may help to secure Kyle's adoption for her but she wished there'd been another way to get Roger to cooperate.

"It's going to be all right," Matt whispered.

"I hope so." She wound her arms around Matt's waist and laid her cheek to his chest. The steady drumming of his heartbeat gave her comfort. They both gazed at the baby they were fighting to keep. He seemed to feel their eyes on him and he blinked at them.

They lingered a moment to bask in the warmth of their makeshift family unit.

Kyle's eyelids lowered ever so slowly, and finally shut. He sighed. The pacifier slid from his mouth.

"And he's out," Matt whispered. He exerted just enough gentle persuasion with his arm to turn her toward the door.

Matt pulled the door half-shut behind them. In the brightly lit hall, Dani moved slightly away from him.

He squared his shoulders.

She fiddled with the ends of her hair.

He started to say something stupid about how badly he'd played golf. But at the last second he stopped himself. If she asked why he'd done so miserably he had no idea what he'd say. After all, admitting he'd lost all semblance of concentration because he kept envisioning her in that naughty lingerie would make them both feel more awkward. If it were possible for them to feel any more awkward than they already did. He cleared his throat.

Dani crossed and uncrossed her arms over her red-and-white Indiana University T-shirt. She, too, seemed ready to speak. But then, nothing.

Finally they both blurted something out in unison.

"Did you heat up the pizza?"

"What happened with Kyle today?"

Dani gave a startled laugh. "Which should we talk about? Pizza or Kyle?"

"Kyle." Matt winced. "Definitely Kyle."

Dani sighed and shook her head. Tension darkened her beautiful features. "Kyle's gums are swollen again and he's been a little bear. And as if it wasn't enough that I had to hear it from you, Mom thinks that because of his circumstances, I need to plan on staying home with Kyle, too."

Matt practically bit through his tongue to keep from shouting his relief at having such a powerful ally.

"Didn't you hear what I said?" she asked, her toe tapping on the soft carpet.

"I heard." He kept his court face on.

"You heard? That's it? No gloating? No rush to reinforce the opinion?" She waved her hands in the air, as her voice escalated in intensity. "No primitive display of masculine superiority?"

He leaned over her. "What did you have in mind? Shall I light a bonfire in the backyard and dance around it naked?"

Her eyes widened. She swallowed so hard that Matt could see the movement in her neck. Bull's-eye. Did he know how to hit his target or what? He smiled. Her reaction changed. Her eyes narrowed and Matt braced himself.

"What I had in mind," she said in a deliberate whisper, "was to feel some support from the people who are supposed to care about me."

Matt held up his hand and turned his head. "Dani, I don't want to have this argument right now."

"Oh?" She planted her fists on her hips. "Well, when do you want to have it? I have to give the hospital some notice if I don't plan to return, you know."

"But you don't have to notify them tonight." He raked both hands through his hair and headed toward his own bedroom. "Can't we just let it go until tomorrow?"

"Let it go?" Her voice cracked.

The dull thudding of her feet on the plush carpet told Matt she was right behind him.

"I let it go this morning when you were in a rush. I let it go at lunch when you trashed all the résumés. Now you want me to let it go again?" She drew a shuddering breath. "Letting it go is my old way of dealing with you, but things have changed now."

He paused in the doorway to his room, keeping his back to her as he warned, "You're pushing it, Dani."

She rose on tiptoe to speak to him over his own shoulder. "Well, get used to it because I'm going to go right on pushing it until I'm satisfied."

"Good thing I don't ascribe to the same philosophy or..." He clamped his mouth shut and stepped inside his room.

"Or what?" She followed.

"Don't, Dani."

"No, I want to know." She circled him to confront him eye to eye. "Or what?"

He tried to sidestep her. She maneuvered with him as if she were a mirror image.

She flattened her palm to his chest. "Or what, Matt? It's a good thing you don't ascribe to the philosophy of pushing things until you're satisfied, or what?"

He leaned down to put his face to hers. His eyes, which she'd seen plagued by turmoil all day went deadly calm. "Or I'd have been after you day and night, making love to you every minute in a thousand ways, until you couldn't stand it anymore."

She gasped, dragging in his own warm breath as she did.

"Then we'd lose ourselves in that bed and in each other until we were so satisfied that we could barely talk, let alone go about our normal household duties."

He straightened and tried again to move around her. She blocked him with a determined stance. "So, what's stopping you?"

"What's . . . ?" Tension ticked beneath his smooth jawline. His inner struggle played out in the flashing pools of his eyes.

Dani held her ground. The time was now or never. Whatever would become of them would be decided within the next few thrashing beats of her heart.

Matt shut his eyes. He twisted his head to one side. "Don't play games with me, Dani. This is not some casual flirtation that you can fend off if it gets too hot and heavy."

"I know that," she said with quiet conviction. "Now, tell me, what's stopping you from making love to me until we're both a couple of zombies?"

He shut his eyes as if to blot out the burning brilliance of the sun. "I promised not to try to seduce you."

"As I recall, I made the same promise." She flexed her hand over the gooseflesh on her arm. "But that didn't keep me from making a spectacle of myself at lunch."

"Don't do this," he croaked, his breathing accelerated, "unless . . ."

"Unless what, Matt?" She fought to control her own breathing. "Unless I mean to see it through—all the way?"

"*All* the way," he reaffirmed.

"What if I said I was ready?"

He jerked his head up and his eyes flashed with something between pain and passion.

"Matt, maybe when I dressed up for you at lunch I still wanted to pretend I wasn't trying to seduce you. But I'm not a kid. Deep down, I knew what I was doing." She shook her hair back and tipped her chin up. "I've been dreaming of marrying you, of wearing that kind of lingerie for you, of making love with you for years."

"Oh, Dani." Matt opened his arms to her.

She moved into his embrace, laying her cheek on his chest. "That's a long time to wait for your life to begin."

He cupped her face in his hands. His eyes searched hers. "Tell me, Dani. Tell me what you want from me."

"I want—" she wet her yearning lips and lifted her face to his "—everything."

The word. The kiss. The sizzle of sensation shooting through her body. All demanded her attention. She gave herself over to each—and to the man behind them. Her hands slid inside his shirt to stroke his hot skin. She arched her back, creating an extraordinary friction between his unyielding chest and her supple breasts.

"Dani." He tore his lips from hers. "Don't." His gaze was both searching and distant. His breathing hard but shallow. "Don't do this unless you mean it. I've been too close to the edge of taking you for too long. I don't know if I could stop."

She dug her fingertips into the resilient muscles in his back. Her eyes focused with sharp intent on his. "Then don't stop, Matt."

He dived both hands into her hair and bent her head to rest just below his chin. "Do you know what you're saying, Dani?"

She swallowed hard. Her pulse roared in her ears. She buried her nose in his shirt and inhaled the scent of his after-shave and skin. "I'm saying I think it's time I made love with my husband."

Air whooshed from his lungs. He crushed her hair in his hands. "You don't know how much I want that, too."

She skidded her hands down his spine while rolling her hips slowly across the swollen evidence of his desire. "I have some idea."

Without further warning, Matt wrapped his arms around her and lifted her feet from the floor. Dani giggled at the caveman tactic as he carried her to the waiting bed. But when he lowered her to the mattress her amusement faded and excitement took its place again. She lay back on the soft bed and waited.

Matt stood over her, his face reflecting love and passion. He stripped away his shirt. It fell quietly to the carpet.

Dani pulled away her own T-shirt and flung it to the floor.

Matt pushed his gym shorts down his long legs, then stepped out of them.

Dani slid out of her shorts as well. She moaned her approval as he joined her on the bed.

Capturing her face in his hands, he bore his gaze into hers. The cords of his neck tightened like steel under her own hands. When he spoke, it was through clenched teeth. "I want more than just the physical act, Dani. For years you told me that when we consummated our love, it would be the culmination of everything we'd worked to build in our relationship. We'd belong to each other. Completely. Forever."

"Forever," she echoed, her voice trembling.

He drew her face to his. At first he teased her lips with a flickering of his tongue, then he kissed her fully. She arched her back and answered his passion with her own. His hands caressed her, beginning with her neck then gliding in slow, exquisite exploration down her body.

Heat from his palms penetrated the filmy fabric of her lace bra. His fingers skipped over the tiny rosebud covering the front hook and in a moment the undergarment fell away. Matt tore his lips from hers and bent his head to lightly kiss the pink peaks of her breasts.

She gasped at the delicate sensation. For a split second, she was sixteen again, feeling everything for the first time with the only man she could ever give her heart to. His fingertips strummed downward until they snagged in her silk panties.

Matt lifted his face. She met his eyes. He asked with a look. This time she responded not as a shy sixteen-year-old but as a woman. It was a small effort for him to slip the wispy white panties down her legs, especially since he had her full cooperation. Just as she had his when she curled her fingers in the stretchy material of his briefs and tugged them off.

Seeing him this way for the first time startled her. Then amazed her. Then thrilled her in a million ways she'd never dreamt possible. She smiled and ran her hand down his side, not quite ready to act on her more lustful impulses. Matt groaned and leaned close enough to nuzzle her ear.

She clutched his shoulders, pulling him closer, urging him over her. He fit his knees between hers. The coarse hair of his muscular legs chafed at her smooth inner thighs. She bit her lip to keep from moaning in pleasure and anticipation.

He dipped his head to drop tiny kisses along her neck. She inhaled the fresh scent of lingering shampoo and Matt's warm skin. His mouth trailed over her jawline, up to her cheek, then down again to claim her lips.

She kissed him eagerly, baring her need for him. Her hands were everywhere, roaming down the length of his spine, cupping the tight flesh of his buttocks. His growl of approval resounded in her ears. His tongue probed the plump center of her lower lip, then plunged inside her mouth.

Dani cried out as their bodies imitated the intimacy of their kiss. To her surprise, the pain she had expected was slight compared to the rapture she felt. She gasped for air, her breath coming in ragged puffs as Matt moved inside her. A blissful sense of belonging interwove with the pure physical force building within her. Aware of even the tiniest detail of Matt's body—the texture of his skin, the softness of his lips murmuring against her temple, the wanton rhythm of his rocking into her—she lost herself in the moment.

"I've waited so long for this," Matt said in a husky tone that teetered on desperation. "I don't think I can hang on much longer...."

Dani exhaled a shuddering breath, whispering, "Then just let go, sweetheart."

The power of Matt's release sent wondrous waves rippling through Dani's body. She clung to him, riding out the tide. When it subsided it seemed to drain every last ounce of energy she possessed. Matt stretched out alongside her and cuddled her close. But she could not keep herself from slipping into a gratified, groggy state.

"Hey, sleepyhead, don't you know it's the man who's supposed to roll over and doze off?" He brushed his fingertips over her cheek. A faint smile touched her lips. Matt laughed. "Of course you don't know that. How could you?"

She hummed a vague response, her eyes still closed.

"But maybe you do know what this meant to me. Do you realize that no other woman has ever mattered to me the way that you do? No one ever will." He searched her placid face for any hint that she heard and understood his confession. Nothing but drowsy satisfaction greeted his gaze. He lightly nudged her shoulder. "Dani?"

"Hmm?"

He leaned over and stared into her face. No trace of emotion lingered there. A dull ache settled into his gut. All the expectations he had once held for this moment taunted him. Could it be that Dani no longer vested the act of making love with special meaning? Could he have hurt her so badly that giving herself to him was no longer any more significant than giving herself to Roger Grant—as she would have if she'd married the jerk?

He shook his head, not wanting to believe the evidence before him. He poked her arm with one finger. "Dani? Isn't there something you want to say to me? Don't you want to tell me what you feel?"

"Hmm."

"Well?"

"Ba fava voo," she murmured, then rolled onto her side, putting her back to him.

"Ba fava voo? What the hell does that mean?" He lay back against his pillow, turning the strange garbled phrase over in his mind.

What had Dani tried to tell him before she fell into her deep sleep? "Fava? Did you mean father?"

She sighed.

Had she tried to tell him she thought of him only as Kyle's father? After what they had just shared? Matt shook his head. His heavy heart would not allow that to be the only answer he considered. He tried again to piece the puzzle together. "Ba fava voo. I'm fond of you?"

She snuggled her cheek to the plump feather pillow.

"I..." If he said it aloud, would it give him too much to hope for? Would he only be deluding himself so that he could postpone the pain of their relationship drifting apart after the custody case was settled? He didn't care. There was another credible interpretation for Dani's nonsensical mumbling. He drew a deep breath and whispered the question to his sleeping wife. "Dani, is it possible you said 'I love you'?"

Of course, she didn't answer. And Matt didn't ask again that night, even though they made love three more times. It wasn't that he didn't want with all his heart to know how she felt about him. He just wasn't sure how he would cope if the answer she gave wasn't the one he needed to hear.

Chapter Nine

Dani tucked the balled-up pillow under her head. In her half dream state she could almost feel Matt's warm breath tickling the hairs on the back of her neck. She eased a satisfied sigh through a lazy smile.

Making love with Matt had been everything she'd ever hoped or imagined. He'd been both gentle and demanding. And when their bodies melded together a deeper union resulted. The entwining of two souls, the healing of past wounds, the promise of forever; she'd felt them all in that one magical moment.

She giggled, deciding to wake her husband in the same sweet way he had roused her just a few hours ago. "Oh, Matt...?" she cooed, rolling over. "Matt?"

She blinked at the empty space beside her in the rumpled bed. As though her eyes were lying to her, she thrust her hands out to pat down the cool sheets where her husband should have been. The crackle of paper startled her. She snatched up the neat white rectangle lying on Matt's pillow.

"'Dear Mrs. Taylor,'" she read aloud. *Mrs. Taylor.* She was furious at Matt for not being here when she woke up, but how she loved hearing herself called Mrs. Taylor and knowing it applied in every way. She drew her legs up and placed the note on the table created by the sheet over her knees.

"'Wish I were there beside you,'" she continued to read. "'But I'm afraid I have to attend to some pressing business this morning.'"

Business. Dani tensed at the word, but she made herself read on. "'Sorry to rush off. I hope you understand. I've broken my back trying to arrange an important meeting and when I checked with the office this morning—'"

Bitterness burned at the back of her throat. When would Matt ever change? Could he change? Tears sprang into her eyes. She'd been a fool to think he could.

She swiped away the droplets blurring her vision. Her chest constricted, but somehow she found enough air to finish the note. "'What happened last night was the culmination of a lifetime of longing. And it is because of that, that I feel compelled to tackle this new project. Please believe me, it will pay off in the long run.'"

"'Because of that . . .'" Translation: Now that Dani had surrendered to him. "'I feel compelled to tackle a new project.'" He no longer had to put up the pretense that his obsession with work would take a back seat to his wife and family. "It will pay off in the long run." Dani rolled her eyes. "There's that tired old refrain about achieving total financial security."

She crumpled the page in one fist without reading the signature. How could he do this to her? How could the man she thought she loved, the man she had given herself to without reservation, do this?

Dani wrapped her arms around her knees and hugged them close. The only thing that kept her from sitting there and sobbing like a baby was the real baby wailing from across the hall.

Kyle. Dani got out of bed and dressed quickly. From this moment on, she would never again lose sight of the reason she had married Matt. For Kyle. To keep him as her son. Toward that end, she would be a good wife to Matt in spite of his distraction with work. She would be pleasant. She would even enjoy the physical side of the relationship. Hadn't she prepared herself to do as much with Roger?

She marched from the bedroom where she and Matt had shared so much—that now counted for so little. As she crossed the threshold, she made a silent vow. She would do whatever it took to keep Kyle. But she would never forget the rude awakening she had received this morning. She would never let her guard down with Matt Taylor again.

Matt tiptoed into the darkened bedroom. He didn't need the light to find his way to the huge bed where he could see the form of his sleeping wife. No, slipping in after nightfall had become second nature to him these past few days. Still, Dani had never scolded him for the late hours.

He gazed down at her, curled up in their bed. Had he thanked her yet for being so understanding? A hungry smile curved his lips upward. He thanked her time and time again each night and she, in turn, had made him feel like the most virile man alive. He tugged at the waistband of his ever-tightening pants. Her cooperation made it tempting to let her in on his grand scheme.

Dani stirred. Matt held his breath. She mewed softly, turned on her side to face him, then sighed. No, he couldn't risk telling her anything about his future plans. Not until he was absolutely certain he could pull it off. If he let her down one more time, that would be the end of their marriage. He had no doubt whatsoever of that.

He looked at her again. Now that his eyes had adjusted to the light, he could see the subtle shading of the moonlight over her features. The way it shimmered off the dark curls clinging along her temple and down her inviting neck. Matt wet his lips and sank to the bed. In a heartbeat, his mouth met the tantalizing hollow above her collarbone.

"Oh!" Dani jumped.

Matt raised his head to meet her bleary gaze. "Hi."

"What time is it?" She sat up and yawned.

He found himself yawning, too, as he checked his watch. "It's about nine-thirty. Sorry to be so late. The person I was supposed to interview got lost trying to find Woodbridge. That threw the whole schedule off."

Dani rubbed her eyes. "Kyle fussed all day. Teething." She groaned and threw her hands up in frustration. "When he finally conked out for the night, I couldn't resist sneaking in a few winks myself."

"Hey," he said, tugging at his necktie. "You don't have to justify needing to catch up on your rest to me." He winked at her. "I happen to recall how you lost all that sleep in the first place."

Dani skimmed her teeth over her lower lip, and stretched, recklessly displaying every sexy contour of her body for his enjoyment. "I'm not sleepy now, you know."

He smiled and took her in his arms. "I'm not sleepy, either. But before we tire ourselves out again, I need to tell you something."

"Okay." She nuzzled his crisp white shirt. "And I have some news for you, too."

"You first." He wrangled with the Windsor knot in his dark, patterned tie.

Dani took over the task, her fingers working the fabric free with ease. "I got a call today from the hospital."

"Oh?" He tensed.

"The school nurse who has been substituting for me, would like to keep on working full-time through the summer."

"Oh?" He relaxed a little.

"Uh-huh." She pulled the tie away and tossed it on the floor. "They wanted to know if I would be interested in extending my leave of absence—without pay, of course—until September."

"Oh." The tension returned to his body. He braced himself for the answer.

She popped open the top button on his shirt, then proceeded down the row. "I told them..." She reached the waistband of his charcoal-colored pants. Using both hands, she tugged his shirttail loose. "I told them I thought it was a perfect solution."

Matt let out a whoop and grabbed her. Together, they toppled to the mattress. He pulled her to fit along his side and planted tiny kisses on her face.

"I guess this means you approve of my decision to spend more time bonding with the baby." She threw her head back, guiding his head toward that tender spot she so loved for him to kiss along the side of her neck.

He hit the spot and she sucked air in through her teeth, her whole body writhing with delight.

"I suppose it's chauvinistic of me to feel so happy about this," he said between nibbles. "But we just have such unique circumstances. Kyle really needs all the time we can give him to adjust."

"All the time *we* can give him," she parroted. "Does that mean you, too, Mr. Been-getting-home-long-after-the-baby's-bedtime?" She furrowed her fingers into the thick tumbles of his hair.

The gentle chiding tweaked Matt's sensibilities. He pulled away from her. "Hey, I'm doing this for you and Kyle."

"Oh well, take it from me, if we had to choose between having you around and having a few more dollars in the bank, we'd pick you almost every time." She smiled at him and tried to coax him back to her.

Matt resisted her prompting just as he resisted joining her in her good humor. "Dani, I understand the importance of being available to my family. I wish I could make you believe me when I say that I have every intention of providing that—soon. But not until I can be sure that..." He ran one hand back through his hair and tried a different tack to reach her. "Do you have any idea how much it costs a year to provide for a child?"

She rolled her eyes in comic exasperation. "Oh, I'd say it would cost a fraction of what you paid for that urban assault vehicle sitting in your driveway."

Matt opened his mouth to argue, then shut it. He crossed his arms over his chest.

Dani laughed and tugged at the taut muscles of his forearms to untangle the knot pressed squarely against his puffed-up chest. "You've done well, Matt. It's okay to relax and enjoy the fruits of your hard work."

He shook his head, letting his arms slacken under her touch. "Dani, you just don't realize how precarious life is. Things happen. Just think of Karen and Bill."

Dani lowered her eyes for a moment. When she raised her head, a softness glowed in her eyes. "I don't think it's what happened to Karen and Bill that's driving you, though, Matt. You're running from the ghosts of your own childhood."

Matt sighed. "You just don't know what it was like, living the way we did. Having everyone in town either snickering at you or feeling sorry for you."

"I don't remember anyone laughing at or pitying you, Matt Taylor. You were like...like the embodiment of every small town dream." She looked away, her head cocked.

"The first time you asked me out, I thought I'd died and gone to heaven. I was the envy of every girl in high school."

"Even though I never had the cash to take you anyplace nice?"

Dani shrugged. "We were in Woodbridge, Matt. The only real restaurant we had then was in the hotel. My daddy would have skinned you alive if he'd ever seen your beat-up old Mustang parked outside that place when you were on a date with me."

Matt laughed.

"Besides—" she moved closer and slipped under his arm "—every time you held me, I was in the nicest place in town."

"You were?"

"Yep." She nestled into his embrace.

He wanted to ask her if she still felt that way, but before he could, she playfully nipped his chin. He lowered his head and growled, "If that's so, then allow me to take you there again."

She lay back and wiggled her body into position under his. "First, tell me your news."

"Mmm?" He pressed his mouth to her ear. His tongue flicked out to tease the sensitive shell.

She caught her breath. "You said you had to talk to me about the case. If it's important, you'd better tell me now, before we lose all interest in verbal communication."

"It's not all that important." He pushed up the hem of her purple satin nightgown.

The fabric slithered over her smooth skin and Dani moaned in anticipation.

"I just wanted to let you know," he made himself say before things got any hotter, "that the Delaneys pulled another no-show for their last appointment."

"That's good." She practically panted the words. "Is their lawyer through with them?"

"I don't know. I couldn't get in touch with Wayne. I heard about the Delaneys from your old pal." The pads of his fingertips formed to the rise of her breasts beneath the gown.

She arched her back to press herself to him. "What pal?"

"Roger Grant."

The name had the effect of a bucket of ice water on her libido. She shoved his hands away from her body and sat up. "Roger? You talked to Roger about the case?"

"It was no big deal." He sat up, his own desire drained by the intrusion of the distasteful memory. "Our paths crossed in the courthouse. He made a snide remark, I set him straight. We exchanged a few barbed comments about the case. No bullets, no bloodshed."

She pushed the hem of her gown down. "What did he say? What did *you* say?"

Matt scowled. He rubbed his hand along his jaw. "If you have to know, he made a rather crude remark about my manhood, which I dismissed. Then he made an uncalled-for reference to what he could have offered you in a 'real marriage.'" Matt rolled onto his back and stared up at the ceiling. "Damn it, Dani, when he brought you into it, I couldn't ignore him."

She laid one shaking hand on Matt's chest. "What did you say?"

"Without stooping to his level, I made it very clear that we had a real marriage in every sense of the word." He notched his fingers with hers and turned to smile at her. "That we intended to make our marriage work—and that we intended to adopt Kyle."

She pulled her hand free, using it to rake through the curls falling over her stiff shoulders. "Then what did he say?"

"What difference does it make?" Matt sat up, ready to put an end to the whole conversation. "He was only blow-ing smoke. I let him know I knew there was nothing he could do to affect the case at this point.''

"Do you believe that?" She pressed her cold palm to the skin exposed by his open shirt. "Did he?"

"He made some childish remark implying I'd find out how much damage he can do." He took her face in his hands and placed his forehead to hers. "But, sweetheart, he has no influence in this case. Believe me. There's nothing he can do to hurt our chances of winning Kyle."

He folded her into a tight embrace, needing to reassure her. She laid her head on his shoulder and whispered, "I only pray that you're right, Matt."

Dani checked her watch once again. The court proceedings seemed to have been dragging on forever with no indication of when they would end—or who would win. Apparently Sarah and Veronica had gotten their act together in the eleventh hour and come up with a viable argument for being granted custody of Kyle. Prodded, no doubt, by Roger Grant.

Their lawyer, Wayne Perry, was quite competent. He built a fairly convincing case for the Delaneys. The reports he cited from the child welfare worker in Ohio called conditions in both Delaney households excellent. He offered three character witnesses apiece for the women. Then, both Sarah and Veronica spoke eloquently about the importance of family and of giving the baby a sense of personal history— for medical and psychological reasons.

Matt had conceded the importance of both of those things—and pointed out that as adoptive parents, they would never rob their child of his heritage. Then, in a few short questions he totally discredited the women's claims of the strength of their family ties. Systematically, he had gotten them to confess that they had neither seen the baby, nor known any pertinent facts about him, until the custody case arose. Each woman recounted the details of Bill Delaney's fall from grace with the family that now so wanted to take in his son. And in a stroke of pure luck, Matt had stumbled on a line of questioning that led to a very incriminating bit of evidence. Sarah Delaney let it slip that she had been the one to send Kyle's court-appointed guardian to Woodbridge in search of "Karen's people."

Matt was brilliant. And if anything else had been at stake, Dani would have reveled in watching him work. But this was all getting too nerve-racking. She gnawed her lower lip and clasped her hands in her lap to keep from fidgeting.

Sarah and Veronica, she noted, appeared calm and unruffled. When Matt handed Judge Harcourt a glowing report from the state social worker who had visited their home, neither woman batted an eyelash. When he followed that with affidavits from friends, family and professionals attesting to their character and to their potential as parents, Sarah had actually yawned. During Dani's heartfelt testimony, Veronica had popped a peppermint candy into her mouth.

When Dani had concluded, Wayne Perry stood and asked the court's indulgence. It seemed a witness whose input would prove pivotal to rendering a fair decision, was late. Judge Harcourt allowed that they would wait five minutes, no longer.

Dani leaned over to Matt and pointed to the Delaney sisters under the table. She whispered, "Those two act like they couldn't care less about this whole thing."

"Or like they're sure they're going to win," he answered in a low, concerned tone. He shook his head. "I'd give anything to know in advance what trick they have up those designer sleeves."

They're sure they're going to win. After that, nothing Matt said registered. Could they? Was it even remotely possible? They were so wrong for Kyle. They didn't love him. They didn't deserve him. Surely the judge would see that.

She lifted her eyes to Judge Harcourt's kindly face and saw his features darken. With dread, she turned in the direction the judge was staring, just in time to see Roger Grant enter the courtroom.

"No." The word blew silently across her lips. Her hand shot out to grip Matt's arm.

"Your Honor, I object." Matt rocketed to his feet. "This witness is irrelevant."

Wayne Perry stood slowly, pushing his chair back with an irritating screeching sound. "What I believe Mr. Taylor wanted to say was that this witness's testimony is irrelevant."

Wayne glanced at Matt, who answered his colleague with a withering glare. He'd said exactly what he'd meant and he wanted Wayne, the court and especially Roger Grant to know it. When the courtroom clock had ticked off enough silence to make his point, Matt gave Wayne a curt nod. "Your Honor, this witness has nothing relevant to add to these proceedings."

"I will prove to you, Your Honor, that this man has information relevant to the nature of the home that the Taylors intend to provide the Delaney child."

Matt's gaze shot through Dani like an arrow. She lifted her shoulders to tell him she didn't know what Roger's information could be. But at the last second she paused, killed the gesture and dropped her gaze.

His stomach sank. He turned away from her. "If it pleases the court, in light of this new development, we ask for a brief recess."

"Well, I . . ." Judge Harcourt coughed. "Mr. Perry?"

"No objection, Your Honor."

"Will ten minutes be enough?" the judge asked Matt.

"Yes, Your Honor."

"This court will reconvene in ten minutes," Judge Harcourt announced.

Purposeful chaos ensued the judge's departure. In a matter of moments, Matt had Dani by the arm and had spirited her off to a secluded spot in the hallway.

"What the hell is Roger Grant going to say about us?" he demanded.

She fell back against the wall. Her pretty face paled to rival the gray of the marble at her back, her green eyes dulled to the same mossy shade of the suit she wore. Matt flattened his palm to the smooth, icy surface behind her, his arm straight. This both created an intimate shelter for their discussion and made it easy for him to catch her if she should get weak in the knees.

"Dani, if you have any idea what Grant might say, you have to tell me," he said with quiet control.

"Well, there are the rumors he's been spreading."

"Wayne Perry is too good a lawyer to haul Grant into court without something concrete." He lifted her chin with his free hand. "Do you know what it could be?"

"Oh, Matt." Tears shimmered above her dark lashes. "I . . . I let Roger think that you and I weren't going to stay married."

"You what?"

"It was before we . . ." She strangled on the words.

"Made love?"

She nodded. A tear broke free from her lashes and fell onto his hand. The warm droplet pooled in his palm. He choked back his own emotion.

"Tell me what happened, Dani."

"I ran into Roger right after we came back to Woodbridge." She paused to swallow and wipe away another tear. "I had to stop him from messing up the custody case."

He splayed his fingers on the cold marble wall. "So you told him we were ending our marriage?"

"No." She raised her head in honest immediacy. "No, Matt. He said that. I just let him believe it was true."

His jaw tightened until he doubted he could have uttered a complete sentence. "Anything else?"

"I promised him a date after you and I split up."

He whispered a curse.

"Matt, this was all before we really committed ourselves to making our marriage work. I would have said anything to help my case for keeping Kyle. Surely Judge Harcourt would understand . . ."

"Judge Harcourt?" He barked a cruel laugh. "Judge Harcourt, the man who pulled strings to get us married? The man who all but told us our only chance of getting custody was as a married couple?" His spine jerked into an unyielding line. He spread his arms wide. "Oh, yeah, I'm sure if we walk into that courtroom and explain how you only married me to get a better footing in the custody case, he'll understand perfectly."

"He might, if we laid it all out for him, apologized and told him how drastically things have changed."

"Dani, do you have any idea what kind of man Evan Harcourt is? What kind of man would manipulate circumstances in a case to appeal to his own sense of whimsy?"

"You said he was decent and fair."

A humorless chuckle burst through Matt's tight lips. "Yeah, decent and fair, with an ego twice as big as his size forty-four belly. He won't take lightly, having testimony in his own court that he's been played for a fool."

"But we didn't . . ."

"And how will it look for me?" he continued. "When it comes out that my wife only married me to further her own agenda? My reputation will be shot."

She shifted her feet and her heels skidded with a screech on the hard marble floor. "Your reputation? As a lawyer or a lover?"

"As a lawyer." He sneered. "I'm going to have to go into the courtroom where I worked for years to establish myself as an honest advocate of the law and hear my wife's ex-fiancé imply I knowingly let you mislead a judge for personal gain."

"Lower your voice," she pleaded. "And drop that righteous act. You're every bit as guilty as I am of marrying under false pretenses."

His hands plummeted like lead to his sides. "I don't know what hurts more, the fact that you're so cavalier about your motives or that you honestly believe what you're saying about me."

"What do you mean?" She tossed her hair off her shoulders. "You were the one who told me that our marriage needn't be a permanent solution to my problem."

"Because anytime you want out, I'll let you go, Dani. I wouldn't hold you in a marriage that made you unhappy." He shook his head.

"Then you didn't just marry me to help me keep Kyle?"

"Dani." He took her hand. "I built a house to make a home for you and our family. I built a career to support that family. When I took my wedding vows..." He cleared his throat to chase away the husky hints of telltale emotion. "I meant them."

"Oh, Matt." The tears spilled onto her cheeks. "I've treated you so unfairly. All I could think of was how I could hold on to Kyle. I completely ignored your feelings."

His mouth twitched. He pinched her chin between his thumb and forefinger. "That's not exactly true. These past few days—and nights—you've paid quite a bit of attention to my feelings."

"Shh!" She put her finger to her lips. "This isn't the time or place."

"Why?" He closed in on her until he could feel the heat of her blushing cheek washing over his lips. "You think it

will shock anyone in this courthouse that two honeymoon-
ers have been enjoying their new sexual relationship?''

''Matt, stop.'' She pushed halfheartedly at his chest.
''Honestly, sometimes you drive me crazy.''

''Only sometimes? He corralled her by placing his hands
on either side of her head. Angling his face over hers, he
whispered, ''You drive me crazy every waking minute—and
most of the sleeping ones, too.''

''Not now, Matt.'' She slipped her mouth out from under his. ''This isn't helping us a bit.''

''Actually it's doing me a world of good.''

''But it's not giving us any solutions to our problem.''

That verbal reality check made him straighten up—literally. He stuffed his hands into his pockets and frowned as
he summed up the situation for her. ''Unfortunately our
problem only has one viable solution.''

''And that is?''

''We have to keep Roger Grant from testifying.''

Her eyes grew big with horror. ''How?''

''We have to stop the hearings.''

''Can we do that?''

Matt shrugged. ''We can try. In light of this new evidence, I should be able to get a postponement.''

Dani shut her eyes and sighed in relief. ''Good.''

''Maybe not so good.'' He grabbed her by the shoulders
and gave her a shake. ''I want you to understand going in,
Dani, that in granting the postponement the judge may
change the temporary custody arrangements.''

She clutched his arms. ''Why? Why would Judge Harcourt do that?''

''Because we've had Kyle up until now. In all fair-
ness . . .''

''No.'' She pushed at his chest. ''You can't let them take
my baby, Matt.''

"Me?" Matt's shoes scuffed the marble floor as he retreated a step. "I can't stop them. If that's the decision of the court, we will have to abide by it."

Desperation churned in her eyes. "Then make sure it's not the decision of the court. You're the best lawyer in town, Matt. Don't let them take Kyle."

"Dani, I'll do my best. But you have to be reasonable. I can only do so much."

"*Can* only do so much or *will* only do so much?"

"Dani, get a grip on yourself." He seized her by the upper arms. "You're implying things you don't really mean."

"Oh, I mean them." She plucked his hands from her arms. "Now that we've made love, you no longer think you need Kyle to keep me in this marriage."

"Where did you get a crazy notion like that?"

"From you." Her body radiated tension. She looked up at him through narrowed eyes. "Your actions these past few days have made it perfectly clear. The late hours, that old preoccupation with work, the fact that you won't fight for me to keep Kyle."

Matt glanced right and left to check for prying ears. The corridor was deserted. "You're talking nonsense, Dani."

"Wrong." She spun on her heel and stalked away from him, calling over her shoulder, "I'm not talking at all."

He followed on her heels, then snatched her by the upper arm. "If anyone is acting like they want to blow this custody case, it's you, Dani. If we don't show a united front now, we'll lose for sure."

Dani stifled a sob. "I won't part with Kyle, even for a visitation. There has to be another choice."

"There might have been if Roger Grant hadn't interfered."

"You mean if I hadn't said what I said to Roger, don't you?" She pressed her knuckles to her colorless lips.

"Actually I may be more to blame for his appearance to-day than you are." He hung his head. "What you did wasn't great. But it got him to back off. In turn, Sarah and Veronica's campaign lost the energy it takes to win in court. Then, I antagonized Grant yesterday and suddenly the Delaneys have a case again."

"Oh, Matt." She threw herself into his arms. "Don't make me give Kyle up, even for a while. He needs me."

"I'll try not to let it come to that, Dani, but I can't promise." He plucked the handkerchief from his suit pocket and offered it to her.

She dabbed her red, swollen eyes with the starched, white cloth.

"Even if we do have to let them take Kyle for a short while, it will be all right, though."

"How can you say that?"

"You heard the testimony." He took the hankie from her hand and whisked off a black smudge of mascara on her cheekbone. "Sarah and Veronica might not be the maternal types, but they're not bad people. They'll take good care of Kyle while he's with them."

"This isn't a puppy that we're putting in a kennel while we go on vacation." Her hands bunched his jacket lapels. "This is a baby—my baby."

"Our baby," he reminded her, returning the handkerchief to her.

She tilted her head back, which sent her silky hair tumbling over his hands on her shoulder blades. "If you really felt that way, you wouldn't let him go."

He wanted to shake her. Wanted to shout. But when he looked down into the face he loved so dearly, all he could do was pull her into the safety of his embrace.

"We're talking worst-case scenario, Dani." He stroked her hair. "Let's just play the hand we've been dealt and hope for the best."

The bailiff called for the court to reconvene. Wayne Perry rushed in, conferred with Sarah and Veronica for a few hushed seconds, then whispered something to Matt as he strode toward his chair. He paused. Scowled. Then nodded an agreement.

She wanted to ask what decision had been reached but before she could the bailiff announced Judge Harcourt. The proceedings were under way again.

And almost immediately they came to a standstill. Dani found herself shut out of the interchange over Kyle's destiny when Matt and Wayne Perry were allowed to approach the bench. The two men spoke quietly with Judge Harcourt, who nodded occasionally or asked a question.

After what seemed an eternity, the judge excused them and they returned to their seats.

"What happened?" She grabbed Matt's hand.

He hushed her with a glance.

She gripped the arm of her chair. Her damp palm squeaked against the gleaming wood.

Judge Harcourt coughed. He cast a dubious look at Sarah and Veronica.

Dani's heart lightened.

The judge's bushy brows crimped down over his deep-set eyes. He turned his discerning glare to her.

Her hopes plummeted.

"Well," he began gruffly. "It seems we've had a legal monkey wrench thrown into today's proceedings."

Cut to the chase, Dani thought. Her gaze was riveted to the old man's face. Announce your decision.

"And since it is the desire of this court to render an equitable judgment, which will reflect the best interests of the minor child, Kyle Matthew Delaney, I am willing to allot the two parties more time to prepare their cases."

That was good, wasn't it? Dani held her breath.

"And in doing so, do now order these proceedings to continue two weeks from today. I further expect both parties to act in good faith and do hereby grant the request of Sarah and Veronica Delaney for visitation rights."

Dani gasped.

"Sarah and Veronica Delaney." Judge Harcourt went on. "You are granted the responsibility for the infant until the next court date. Failure to return said infant on or before that time will result in felony warrants being issued against you. Do you understand?"

"Yes, Your Honor," Sarah answered.

"Yes, Your Honor." Veronica's voice boomed confidently over her sister's.

Judge Harcourt turned to them. The tears streaming down Dani's cheeks must have affected him. He paused. Coughed. Paused again, and then said in that kind grandfatherly way of his, "Matthew and Danielle Taylor, you will hand the child over to Sarah and Veronica Delaney by 6:00 p.m. tonight. Do you understand?"

Six? That was only two hours away. Dani pursed her lips to launch an argument. Matt's firm hand on her shoulder kept her still.

He answered for both of them. "We understand, Your Honor."

The judge nodded. "Any action that goes in contrast to the agreements set out by the two sides today, will be weighed thoroughly in future hearings."

The banging of his gavel was as frightening and as final as a gunshot.

Dani rushed outside the courthouse with Matt close behind.

"Slow down, will you?" he called out.

"How can I slow down? I only have two more hours with my baby. I'm not going to waste one second of it."

He caught her by the arm. She yanked to free herself but to no avail. She had to face him.

"Calm down, Dani." He shook her shoulders gently. "This is only temporary. Haven't you ever heard the expression, we lost the battle, but we'll win the war?"

"Haven't you ever heard the expression, once burned, twice shy?"

"What's that supposed to mean?"

"It means, Matthew Taylor, that I trusted you once but that's one mistake I'm never going to make again."

Chapter Ten

Matt curled his hand around the single dart spearing the pocked cork center of its target. He yanked hard. The dart held fast, bringing the whole board with it before finally coming free. The board fell back and bounced twice. The banging jarred loose two stray darts dangling from the den wall. Never had Matt missed the mark so completely.

And my dart game is off, too. Matt dragged the dart over his palm. The clipped feathers hissed through his circled fingers. Nothing he did, he mused glumly, seemed to help his situation with Dani. She didn't want to talk about the strain not having Kyle put on their fragile new relationship. Yet when he respected that and granted her silence, she accused him of being callous to her pain and uninterested in getting Kyle back.

Getting Kyle back. It seemed everything in their household had come to revolve around that one theme. And as much as Matt wanted to help insure that they kept Kyle, he also realized that this constant obsessing was not healthy for Dani or for their relationship.

He strode across the den, wondering what more he could do to help the woman he loved. What Dani needed, he reasoned, was something to get her mind off it, if only for an hour or two.

Exactly. He shut one eye, aimed the brass-tipped dart and hurled it in a triumphant burst of energy. The instant it left his hand, Dani entered the room.

The sinister-looking projectile whizzed by her at eye level. She jumped. "Oh, my gosh."

"Watch out," Matt cried, rushing toward her. The dart pierced the board the same moment Matt reached Dani. "Are you okay?"

She blinked up at him. "Um, yes, just a little startled." She laid her hand over her heart. "I was upstairs reading. I guess I didn't hear you come home." She walked over to the bookcase and replaced a slender volume. "It must be later than I thought. Maybe I should start dinner."

Matt blocked her from leaving the room. "Dinner? At two o'clock in the afternoon?"

"Two?" She snatched up his arm and scanned his wristwatch. "What are you doing home at two in the afternoon?"

Matt shrugged. "Court got out early and I didn't see any reason to hang around the office."

She dropped her jaw in an exaggerated expression of amazement. "Quick, turn on the TV."

"Why?"

"So we can find out just exactly when hell froze over." She crossed her arms.

If she had laughed, Matt would have joined her. But her bitterness cut him to the quick. At last, the tension of these few days without Kyle made him snap. "I've got news for you, Dani. It isn't hell that's frozen—it's your heart."

Tears sprang to the edge of her eyes and trembled there. "That's a lie. My heart is broken not frozen. If anyone is acting coldhearted, it's you, Matt Taylor."

"How?" he demanded. "I don't see that at all."

"You don't see it because you don't pull your nose out of your work long enough to see anything." She shook back her hair. It snagged on the collar of her sleeveless shirt. She yanked it free with venomous vigor. "If we do get Kyle back, what kind of example will you be setting for him?"

Matt moved to the dart board, clutching the two unthrown darts in his fist. "Hopefully I'll be instilling in him a valuable work ethic."

"Work isn't an ethic for you, Matt, it's your reason for living."

"Wrong." He stabbed the two darts into the cork target. "You and whatever family we may have, including Kyle, are my reasons for living—and my reasons for working so hard."

She shook her head. "What are you talking about?"

"About supporting my family, about feeding and clothing my children and keeping a roof over their heads." His volume escalated with each example.

"Oh, Matt." Weariness made her breathy voice tremble. "When are you ever going to realize that you've done enough and let it be?"

"I want to believe that, Dani." He hung his head. "But you know how I was raised. We never knew when Dad came home if he'd have a paycheck or a handful of magic beans." He gave an acid chuckle. "I swore I'd never put my own family through that."

"And what chance is there that you will?" She moved closer to him and tipped her head up to force him to look into her kind, green eyes. "Have you ever once thrown away a whole month's pay investing in a suspicious get-rich-quick scheme?"

Matt shook his head. He pressed his lips together, fighting the painful memories her reference brought to the surface.

"Have you ever, in your entire adult life, had to hide in your car to avoid a bill collector? Quit a job because it interfered with your life-style? Owed money to every friend you ever made?"

Again the memories flooded over him. Again he shook his head.

"And you never will." She laid her hand on his tensed arm. "You've proven to everyone in town that you're not your father, Matt. When are you going to accept it yourself?"

As a lawyer, he had to admit she'd made her case. But that little boy who saw the anguish in his mother's eyes and felt the humiliation of poverty couldn't surrender so easily.

"Trust me, honey, the more hours I put into my present project, the better the possibility for me to slack off in the future."

"By that time Kyle, and any other children we might have, will have children of their own." She dropped her hand. "I wish you'd give me some credit, Matt. I happen to have a few job skills myself. Between the two of us, I think our family could be well taken care of." She threw her hands out to her sides. "Life's a game, Matt, get in it."

Matt skewed his mouth up on one side. "One of those job skills you mentioned wouldn't be writing fortune cookies, would it?"

She answered with a smile. "Okay, so that was corny. But it does apply. You're only given so much time in life, Matt, and you're selling too much of yours for a security that doesn't really exist."

"What if I promised that within the next few weeks I'll cut my workload substantially?"

"If I had a nickel for every time you said that to me, Matt..."

"*You'd* be financially secure, I know." He exhaled long and low. No use in letting her in on his still unsettled strategy—she'd dismiss it as another promise to be broken. No, best to keep his lips sealed until he had something concrete to tell her. "How about if we take it one day at a time, then?"

Dani's expression grew resigned, her eyes sad. "That's about all we *can* do for now."

His heart felt like the center circle of a target and her words the impaling point of a potent dart. All we *can* do, meaning no decisions could be made regarding their future until all was settled with Kyle. His lips twitched to pursue the matter but he caught himself in time. One more word would plunge them back into the downward spiral of speculation over Kyle's future. Right now, their own future as a couple hung in the balance. He had to do something to help make sure they had one.

"Look, it's early and I'm home, what do you say?" He clapped his hands together loudly. "Shall we do something?"

"Do something?" She arched an eyebrow.

"You know, have a little fun?"

"Fun?"

"You mean you've completely forgotten the concept?" He shook his head as he closed in on her. "Has marriage to me been that grim?"

"It's not the marriage, Matt, it's..."

"Kyle," he finished for her. "But it's for Kyle we should do this, Dani."

"For Kyle?" She cocked her head.

"For Kyle," he affirmed, placing a kiss on her adorable little nose. "He deserves to come home to parents who have

a full relationship, not just two people who are only together to make a home for him.''

"I thought we had a little more going for us than that,"
she said, softly.

"Well, we do have *that*." He zeroed in on her and pulled
her to him. "But wouldn't it be nice to have a marriage
based on more than sex and our son?"

The flickering in her eyes told him he'd struck pay dirt.
He dragged her closer, until each breath she took caused her
breasts to skim his chest.

"We had a relationship before we had either of those in
our lives," he whispered. "Can't we rediscover some of
that?"

She put her hands between them and shook her head.
"How?"

Matt tensed his shoulders. "Oh, I don't know. It's a
beautiful summer afternoon. I'm off for the rest of the day.
Maybe we could do something we used to do... you know,
before..."

"Like go swimming?" It was the first time in days Matt
had seen anything pique Dani's interest. Her whole face lit.
Her fingers curled into the fabric of his shirt. She actually
laughed.

"Okay, swimming it is." He tightened his arms around
her. "Do you have a suit?"

"Suit, towels, sunscreen, everything I need and it's all
here at the house. How about you?"

Matt smiled quietly. He planted a quick kiss on her forehead. "Me, too. I've got absolutely everything I need right
here."

The Woodbridge Community Pool was packed when they
arrived half an hour later. Dani searched the sea of bikinis
and beach towels for a vacant spot on the concrete. Prefer-
ably a spot that didn't place Matt smack dab between a
couple of bronzed beauties in brazen swimsuits.

"How about here?" Matt dropped the canvas bag they'd brought on a small square of white-hot concrete.

Three unoccupied towels lay at skewed angles to the left. On the right a man and woman lay, soaking up sunshine as if they'd never heard of ultraviolet rays and premature aging.

"Well . . ." She bit her lip. "I guess this will do."

She had hardly slipped down one shoulder of her lacy cover-up when three giggling girls strolled up to claim their places on the nearby towels. Water beaded on their oiled bodies, and streamed in rivulets down their golden skin. All three paused before settling in to tug and pull and wiggle as though their suits were a size too small.

Dani scanned the scraps of material passing for swimwear. Make that two sizes too small, she amended. "On second thought, this isn't a good spot."

She snatched the canvas bag in one hand and Matt's arm in the other.

"What's wrong with it?" he asked as he dutifully followed.

"It's too . . ." Dani thrust out her lower lip to show she was striving to find just the right word. "Inconvenient."

"Inconvenient?"

She waved her hand in the air. "You know, too far away from some things—" she glanced over her shoulder at the preening teens "—too close to others."

"Yeah," Matt muttered. "I know exactly what it was too close to."

"This is much better," Dani announced when they reached a narrow nook between a half wall and a lifeguard's station.

"Oh, this is perfect," Matt said, stopping to gaze at the long shadow cast by the lifeguard's towering chair.

Dani unfurled her beach towel with a sharp snap, then laid it out on the hard surface. When she had done the same or Matt, they sat down. She peeled off her cover-up and ossed it aside. Matt slipped off his shirt and it joined Dani's clothing in a pile at their feet. She fished a purple bottle of unscreen out of the brightly colored canvas bag and popped open the top.

"Here, let me," Matt said, taking the bottle from her.

"That's not necessary, really." Dani tensed at the notion of Matt's strong hands sliding over her skin to apply the creamy lotion.

"I don't mind," he replied in a husky voice.

"But I can..."

He turned her so that her back was to him. He must have poured the lotion into his hands to warm it because when he licked it over the tight muscles between her shoulder blades it practically melted on contact. And so did Dani.

"Mmm. That's nice. Thank you." She caught her hair up in one hand and held it out of his way.

"You know," Matt said as he slathered on another coat. "I'm the one who should be jealous, not you."

"Jealous?" She twisted around to face him. "What are you talking about?"

Matt nodded toward the girls they had passed. "As far as I'm concerned, you're the most beautiful woman here." He took her arm and started to rub the lotion in, using long, slow strokes. "And I'm convinced that there are plenty of men here who would agree."

Dani shut her eyes and savored the feeling of his hand enclosing her wrist, then gliding upward. How she found the power to smile, much less speak, amazed her. "You're exaggerating my attractiveness a bit, wouldn't you say?"

He moved his attention to her other arm. "No, if anything, I'm understating it."

His palm smoothed up her arm. His fingers curved to caress her shoulder. She bit her lip to keep from moaning in pure pleasure as he moved both hands upward to flatten them against her nape. Then slowly, the pads of his finger slithered down her spine.

"Oooh." Dani shuddered. "You'd better stop that be fore I dissolve."

A low, sexy chuckle rumbled from deep in his chest. Dan swallowed hard and jerked her back taut.

"Your turn." She pulled away from him, grabbed the sunscreen and sat on her knees, waiting for him to comply

"I don't need any sunscreen," he mumbled.

"Stop grumbling, Matthew Thomas Taylor, or I'll be forced to toss you in the pool," she teased.

"You couldn't." He eyed her over his shoulder.

She flexed one arm muscle for him. "Don't bet couldn't."

He laughed his submission, turning his back to her.

Dani globbed a healthy portion of sunscreen into he cupped hand. The coolness of the puddled lotion sent a chil over her entire body. Biting her lip to keep from snickering and giving herself away, Dani slapped the cold goo directly onto Matt's warm skin.

"Yeow!" Matt howled. He dipped his chin to peer at he over his shoulder, grinning. "I thought nurses were sup posed to have a gentle touch."

Dani raised both brows at him and joked, "I can tel you've never been in the hospital."

He scowled at her in mock warning.

She laughed and spread her hands open over his broad back. He relaxed and took his eyes from her. Dani sighed Her palms flexed against Matt's skin. The dollop of lotion liquidized in the heat of her hands, releasing a pungen tropical scent. Suddenly the years, too, seemed to melt away For just that moment, they were teenagers again. Glorying in their youth, the day and each other.

Dani let the slickness of the sunscreen carry her hand down Matt's spine. She moved upward to the broad shoul

ers that proved Matt was no scrawny teen, but a dangerously masculine man. She bit her lip and savored the friction
between his skin and her palm. Touching Matt this way delighted her just as much as having him touch her. She wet
her lips and worked the last of the lotion into his tight neck
muscles.

The act drew her close enough to smell his hair. She shut
her eyes and inhaled, letting her hands slide across the width
of his shoulders and down both his arms. Her fingertips
dipped into the defining valleys of his biceps. She reached
further down along his strong arms, leaning forward until
her cheek brushed his ear and she felt the heat of his body
on her breasts.

"Um, Dani."

His husky voice startled her. Her eyes flew open.

"I think, maybe—" he plucked her hands away and held
them "—it would be a good time for a refreshing and very
cold dip in the pool."

She could only nod her assent.

Matt stood first, then extended his hand to her.

Dani put her hand in Matt's and got to her feet. At the
pool's edge, she dipped her toe in, then shivered. "*Brrr.*
Maybe it's a little too cold for me."

"Aw, don't be like that." Matt gave her shoulders a
squeeze. "You have to jump right in."

"Is that so?" Dani asked, thinking his words were a perfect metaphor for their whole situation. She smiled. "If you
think that's such a great idea, then why don't you go first?"

Matt stuck one foot into the water. He frowned. "On
second thought..."

"Oh, no, you don't. No second thoughts." All it took was
one well-placed shove at Matt's shoulder to send him
sprawling into the chest-high water.

For a moment he disappeared beneath the crystal-clear water. When he came rocketing up from the formerly smooth surface, a wild gleam was in his eyes.

Dani knew it was jump or be dumped. Matt came toward the side of the pool. Just as he reached the edge, she drew a big breath and leapt.

The cold enveloped her. It felt wonderful and awful and invigorating all at once—kind of like life, she thought. She bobbed to the surface and Matt's arms circled her. Together they shook with cold and laughed with joy. For the first time in many days, Dani let herself hope that things might just work out after all.

"This isn't the end of the world, Dani."

"No, but it's the end of my world, Matt." She flattened her hand over her rolling stomach. "It's the end of that sweet little fantasy world I had built for myself with you and Kyle at the center."

Just a few days ago she and Matt reached an uneasy truce at the pool. Since then, they'd tried to work on bettering their relationship in anticipation of Kyle's return. But now...

She spun on her heel and hurried toward the bathroom. Matt's footsteps fell in sync with hers on the plush upstairs carpet. She picked up her pace, rushing through their bedroom to the master bathroom. Before he could stop her she'd slammed the door between them and leaned back. The pristine room dipped and swayed in front of her eyes for a moment until she commanded her jumbled senses to quell.

"Dani, stop this." He pounded the door.

The repeated thuds vibrating against her back only accelerated the throbbing in her head and the swirling in her stomach. She pushed her fingertips to her temples. "No you stop it. Just leave me alone, will you?"

"So you can feel sorry for yourself? I don't think so." He jiggled the doorknob. The lock stopped the knob from turning. "Dani, please. All that has changed is that Sarah and Veronica have filed a countersuit in Ohio. We still have legal custody of Kyle."

"Having legal custody and having Kyle are two different things." She hooked her thumb in the waistband of her brightly patterned shorts. "They can keep him there now, can't they?"

"I can't talk to you through this door. When you're ready to discuss our strategy like two adults, I'll be waiting right over here on the bed."

Dani blew a mild curse through her clenched teeth and rubbed her burning eyes. When she drew her fists away from her face, a haggard woman stared back at her from the bathroom mirror.

She ran her hands through her unkempt curls. Her hair drooped on her shoulders and hung over one eyebrow. Its deep color contrasted with her skin's suddenly pale hue—except for her eyes, which now had bluish purple circles under them.

The headaches, the stomach churning, the sleepless nights. How much more of this could she take? If the Delaney sisters chose, they could drag this out in the courts for months, perhaps years.

All that time hoping Kyle would be theirs for keeps. All that time worrying and wondering, never being able to really get on with her life. How could she stand it?

She had to do something. Once again she had reached a point where she had to take action or let circumstances run roughshod over her. But what was the right thing to do? What was best for Kyle? And for Matt? And for her? Could she find a solution that would be good for all of them? Deep down, she knew there was only one answer.

She ran cold water in the sink, then splashed two handfuls onto her face. The hand towel snapped when she whipped it off the rack. She scrubbed it over her damp cheeks. The rough terry cloth enlivened her skin as it dried it off. She checked her reflection in the mirror again. Better, she thought.

"Okay, Matt." She opened the door and stepped into the bedroom. "I've made up my mind. I know what we have to do."

"You know what to do?" Matt lay across the bed, propped up on one elbow. The legal papers he had shown her earlier lay spread before him. He quirked his mouth up in a half smile. "And what law school did you go to?"

"I don't need a degree to see the right thing to do, Matt." She stepped toward him.

He sat up. "And that is?"

She sat on the bed beside him and met his unrelenting gaze. Her heart fluttered and her throat closed up. Yet, somehow, she found the strength to say what needed to be said. She took his hand and gave it a tight squeeze. "Our only real option now, is to give up Kyle."

Chapter Eleven

"This is a mistake." Dani rolled her head toward the open window in Matt's Range Rover.

"We can turn back." Matt reached across the seat and ruffled the curls along her neck.

"No." She cast her gaze to her lap. "We're half a block from Veronica's house. It would be stupid to turn chicken now."

"I'll do whatever you want." He slowed the Rover to a crawl. "Just say the word."

"No, you say it." She kissed his palm and pulled his hand away from her face. "Tell me one more time the way you think things might work out."

Matt let out a low breath. "Well, my take on the Delaneys is that the last thing they want is to actually have to raise Kyle."

"For people who don't want him, they're sure fighting awfully hard for him."

"They're not fighting at all. They're just baring their teeth." He removed his hand and punched a fist in the air.

"Making a big show of fighting for him for their grandfather's sake."

"I hope you're right." She tried to swallow. Her traitorous stomach rolled.

"Hey." He smiled. "I'm not going to let you go in there and totally surrender Kyle. This is just your chance to let the Delaneys know you're not going to play their game. That you are going to put Kyle's well-being over your own feelings."

She nodded. "I really want to tell them that to their faces."

He pulled into a large circular driveway in front of what would have been considered a mansion in Woodbridge. Dani swallowed hard. Suddenly she understood the magnitude of the battle they were facing with the Delaneys.

"These people could keep us tied up in courts in two states, and wage endless appeals and just consider the expense pocket change."

Matt left the car running, as if he weren't quite certain they were staying. "And all the time, they can blame the system for their lack of success in adopting Kyle."

"Or us," she added glumly.

"Either way, 'Grandpa' is appeased."

She turned to Matt and squinted. "Just how old is their grandfather anyway?"

"Man's got to be in his eighties."

"You don't suppose their plan is to drag the process out just until the old man . . ."

Matt killed the engine. He shook his head. "I don't think either of these ladies is that cold and calculating."

She glanced at the foreboding white house. "This is it, then."

He grabbed her hand and commanded, "Look at me, Dani."

She obeyed with a lump in her throat.

He narrowed his fiery eyes at her. The concentration on his face drew her close, ready to accept his guidance. "Before we go in there, Dani, you have to tell me once and for all if you can live with whatever the outcome may be."

"You mean, if we lose Kyle forever?"

"We've rehashed this from every angle." His jaw ticked with tension. "But I want to hear it from you one final time. Are you prepared to face the possible consequences of our actions?"

The possible consequences. Losing Kyle. In turn, perhaps losing Matt. Because without Kyle there might not be enough of a relationship left to keep them together.

She cast her eyes to the creamy beige upholstery of Matt's Range Rover. To her relief and surprise no tears came this time. Perhaps that was because she'd cried them all out. Or perhaps that's just how it was when you knew you were doing the right thing. She lifted her face. "Matt, putting Kyle through a custody battle between us and his blood relatives might have far-reaching effects that we can't even imagine now."

Matt sighed. "I know."

"And the short-term effects..."

"Being passed back and forth. The trauma of just getting adjusted to one place and then having to relocate," Matt supplied for her.

"Even having to deal with the visitations would be an ordeal."

Matt raised her hand to his lips and placed a kiss there. "Would it all be worth it if it meant we would eventually win the right to adopt him?"

Dani bit her lip to keep her fervent affirmative answer from slipping out. She forced her head to move from side to side. "No. I love Kyle too much to let him spend his formative years that way."

Matt laid his hand on her cheek. She shut her eyes and turned her lips into his warm palm. His other hand flicked a wayward curl from along her temple.

"You're a good mother, Dani. If I never said it before, I want you to know it now."

She felt her mouth form the words thank you into his hand.

"Ready?"

She pulled away from him and squared her shoulders. "Ready."

At the door, Matt gave her hand a quick squeeze and whispered, "This might work in our favor, you know."

She smiled sadly. "I just hope we don't see Kyle. That would really muddy the emotional waters. I don't think I could act my way out of it."

Matt shook his head. "Kyle's with Sarah. We're just seeing Veronica today."

"Why her?"

"Let's just say, I'm playing a hunch."

She wanted to ask more, but before she could the front door swung open.

"Hello, Ms. Delaney," Matt said in that deep, sexy lawyer voice that usually sent Dani's spine shivering.

She wondered if part of Matt's game was flirting with the older woman. She eyed her husband discreetly. A streak of jealousy coursed through her veins. She'd been so focused on "Matt the father" and "Matt the lawyer" these past two days, she'd forgotten to see "Matt the man." She tucked her hand in the crook of his arm as they entered Veronica's home.

"Thank you for seeing us, Ms. Delaney." Matt patted Dani's hand.

Together, they followed Veronica into a sunny room. She indicated for them to sit on an antique love seat. Once she had offered them a drink and brought iced tea for all of them, Veronica dropped the guise of gracious hostess.

"Now, Mr. and Mrs. Taylor." Veronica held her tall, clear glass in the air as though she were about to drink the dark amber liquid. Instead she aimed her no-nonsense gaze at Matt. "Why are you here?"

Matt shrugged. He flashed a blasé smile and leaned back in his seat. "Nothing earth-shattering, we just wanted to clear up a few things about the custody case."

Veronica went rigid. She held her glass suspended high over her tightly crossed legs. "You said this wasn't an official visit."

Matt moved his upper body forward, his hands waving away her concern. "Oh, no. We only want to let you know that we're not going to fight you."

Veronica seemed to remain motionless. But her hand trembled just enough to make the ice clink in her glass. "I beg your pardon?"

"We've made our stand in Indiana." He settled his elbows on his thighs and his gaze on hers. "That's the one and only case we intend to deal with."

"B-but, we've filed our own suit here in Ohio...."

Matt felt Dani's fingers flex into the fabric of the love seat, but his eyes did not move. "We don't intend to contest your case in Ohio."

Veronica's mouth narrowed. She batted her lashes a few times. A bead of water trickled down her iced tea glass and dripped onto her black slacks. She didn't even flinch. "I'm afraid I don't understand."

"It wouldn't be right—for Kyle," Dani blurted out.

Matt glanced over his shoulder at his wife and smiled. "That's the conclusion we've come to, Ms. Delaney."

"Are you saying you're giving up? That you no longer want custody of Kyle?" She sat the glass down on a coaster with a *thunk*.

"Oh, no." Dani edged forward on the seat next to him.

Matt placed his hand on her back and found that the skin exposed by her colorful sundress was damp. He vowed to end this ordeal for her as quickly as possible.

"We still very much want to adopt Kyle," Matt said.

"But we care too much about him to see him dragged through hearings and appeals that don't show any sign of ending." Emotions shimmered in Dani's voice, but she held it together.

"What we want you to understand, then, is that after Judge Harcourt gives his ruling tomorrow, we're through." Matt sliced his hand over the coffee table in front of them. "If we win the right to adopt him and you appeal, or if you pursue a countersuit in Ohio, we'll surrender the baby to you."

"You'd do that?" Veronica's hushed horror targeted Dani.

Don't slack off now, Matt begged her mentally. This is the moment we had hoped to arrive. Don't get sentimental and blow it.

Dani drew herself up. She smoothed her hands down her rib cage, then laced her arms under her breasts. "We are fully prepared to do what's best for Kyle."

Veronica's eyes grew wide. A piece of ice popped in one of the glasses.

Matt fixed a kindly expression on her face and addressed his hostess. "I think you'd be surprised at the amount of support we have for this decision."

"Support?" She said it as if she didn't know the meaning of the word.

"Oh, yes," Dani said, chiming in, sounding more sure of herself as she went on. "Well, everybody has heard those terrible adoption stories where the child is treated like a human Ping-Pong ball and in the end gets torn from one family to be sent to another."

"Yes?" Veronica blinked blankly at her.

"Well..." Dani licked her lips and turned to Matt. He encouraged her to continue with a nod. "Everybody sees how miserable that is for the child...."

"And, of course, there is a certain amount of fallout for the adults—putting a child through that," Matt interjected, his eyes on Veronica's face.

"Fallout?" That got her attention.

"Because it's so unnecessarily cruel," Dani said with earnest passion. "We would never do that to Kyle."

"Oh, I...never considered..."

"We can only hope this mess won't alienate any of your friends." Matt folded his hands together, sat back and leveled his best cool-but-intimidating gaze on her. "Or family."

"Family?"

He wasn't sure, but Matt thought he saw panic in Veronica's formerly detached expression.

"You and your sister do have other family members, don't you?" Matt asked, taking a sip of his iced tea.

"Only a grandfather," she replied in a distracted way.

Matt let the cold liquid bathe his throat before he spoke again. "Then, I suppose, he's in favor of your adopting the baby—to continue the family name."

"Actually he's my mother's father, his last name is Benoit. His daughters married the Delaney brothers." Veronica made the statement into the air, not looking at either of them. "Still, he is in favor of our taking the child in. Family ties, and all that."

"This might be a good time to let you know that if we should win custody, we would stand by our commitment to allow Kyle total access to his family." Matt took Dani's hand to show their unity.

"Would you allow that to be a condition of the adoption?" Veronica arched one eyebrow at them.

"Absolutely," they replied together.

"I see." Veronica rose from her chair. "Well, thank you for bringing me this enlightening information."

Damn. They were being dismissed. Matt had hoped to walk away from this meeting with a more concrete concept of where Veronica stood on the custody issue. Still, they had succeeded in planting the idea in her head to let it go for Kyle's well-being—and ultimately her own.

Matt stood, then reached down to help Dani to her feet. Clearly Dani wasn't ready to walk away but they had to. He flattened his hand on her back to guide her toward the door.

When Veronica reached for the knob, Dani could contain herself no longer. "How has Kyle been, Ms. Delaney?"

"How has he been?" She looked as though she'd been gnawing on a lemon for an instant, but she quickly regained her composure if not her charm. "He's been fine. Wonderful, really. A joy."

"Oh, well . . ." Dani glanced up at him for help.

Matt knew she wanted to ask to see him, but he couldn't condone that. One look at Dani holding Kyle and even Veronica would know that she would fight through hell and back for the baby.

"Thank you for hearing us out, Ms. Delaney."

She dipped her head to him and threw open the door—just as Sarah Delaney came charging up the walk with Kyle wailing in her arms.

"We've lost another nanny, and I have a meeting in half an hour," Sarah bellowed, her view of Dani and Matt precluded by Kyle's thrashing movements.

"Well, well," Matt muttered into Dani's ear. "What have we here?"

The instant Kyle saw Dani and Matt he squealed with delight, which quickly switched to frustration at not being able to get to them. Sarah tried valiantly to calm him but it was obvious she hadn't a clue how to go about it.

Matt turned to Veronica and smiled, "May I?"

Veronica swept her hand out to offer him permission to take Kyle. In a matter of moments, he had scooped up Kyle, kissed him and deposited the quieted baby into Dani's arms. She cuddled him close and began to coo sweet things.

"All right, Mr. Taylor. As you can see, we've had a few problems this week," Veronica admitted.

"A few?" Sarah fanned herself furiously.

Veronica glowered at her sister, then smiled at Matt. "Perhaps we can come to an ... understanding."

"I'm listening."

"Tomorrow, we go back to court. As you probably know, we have a very good case for keeping the baby." She lowered her lashes over a pointed glance at Dani. "You have a case as well."

"Yes?"

"I propose we let that judgment decide the child's fate. Period." She stabbed one brightly polished nail into her cupped palm.

"That's it?" He pushed his suit jacket back and planted his fists on his hips.

"There are some conditions, of course."

"Of course."

"If you win custody, you will agree to grant the family visitation with the child. If you lose, you go away. No further interference with my family."

"And in exchange, you agree to drop the countersuit and not to appeal the court's decision?"

"Agreed."

She extended her hand to shake but Matt held back. "One more thing."

"What's that?"

"Let us take Kyle with us today." He caught Dani's happy, hopeful expression in his sidelong glance. "You have to return him on or before tomorrow anyway."

"This will solve our sitter dilemma," Sarah hissed to her sister.

Veronica closed her eyes and nodded. "Fine. Take him with you."

"I have his bag in my car," Sarah volunteered all too quickly.

They gathered up Kyle's belongings and, in a matter of minutes, were on their way back home as a family again. Dani's face glowed with joy every time she would sneak a peek at Kyle in his car seat. The baby laughed and kicked in sheer contentment.

Only Matt seemed to feel the weight of concern in his chest. He studied the sparkle in Dani's eyes that had not been there since Kyle left and he couldn't help but wonder. If they lost custody of the baby, what would become of their marriage?

Would she continue to share his home—and his bed? A twister of emotion whirled through his being at the thought. Maybe, he allowed himself to speculate, she would stay and in time they would have a family of their own.

Dani—her belly big and round with his baby. His skin tingled. Strange that he should find that image so erotic. He chuckled softly, deciding that was a good omen. He glanced over and caught her making goo-goo eyes at Kyle. His hopes plummeted.

Who was he kidding? If the Delaneys took Kyle out of their lives, he and Dani would have no marriage.

Dani adjusted the cotton collar on Kyle's dressiest outfit, then fit the baby into the crook of her arm. She lifted her head, tossed back her curly brown hair and smiled into the darkness beyond the bright halo of light circling the three of them.

Without disturbing her expression, she whispered, "This was a great idea, Matt, having a family portrait made. It's so symbolic of the fact that, no matter what happens tomorrow, we are a family."

Matt smiled down at Dani and the baby. Secretly he felt like a cad for his out-and-out manipulation of her emotions. By making this last-ditch effort, he'd hoped to fix in Dani's mind once and for all that they belonged together. And by giving her something as tangible as a photograph to take away from it, he would provide something she could not easily forget. He tugged at his navy tie and cleared his throat. "Yeah, well, I'm glad Mr. Mussman agreed to do this sitting for us on such short notice."

"Yes, it was real sweet of him to give up a chunk of his evening for us." She scooted closer to Matt at the photographer's silent suggestion. The old man waved his hand in the air again and she inched closer still. "I just hope we haven't overtaxed him. He may not be up to the stress of working overtime."

"Mussman?" Matt's lips hardly moved as he spoke. "I think he can stand it. He used to take the pictures of every kid from kindergarten to high school in a single day."

"And he doesn't look a day older now than he did then," Dani said, wiggling her eyebrows to show surprise.

"Maybe he's a zombie," Matt teased. "Maybe that's how Woodbridge has survived so long—the town elders zombified every professional in town so we could stay self-sufficient."

"I know one professional they missed." She bit her lip and gazed up at him.

"They tried to get me," Matt said into her temple. "But I'd already been zombified."

"Oh?"

"Yeah, by a beautiful brunette who wanted to keep me as her love slave."

Dani giggled.

"Okay, Taylors," the craggy voice of the town's only photographer, Harold Mussman, called out from the blackness. "Look this way, please. And smile."

The flashbulb exploded like lightning before their eyes. Kyle let out an angry wail. Dani gasped, then immediately started to soothe the child. But above all that, the one sound Matt could hear was the distinct beeping of his pocket pager.

He grit his teeth. Did he dare? A quick glance at Dani told him Kyle wouldn't be settled for a second picture for a minute or two. That would give him just enough time to slip out and answer this call. Maybe Dani wouldn't even notice he'd gone.

She spoke to Kyle in a quiet tone, petting his cheek and bouncing him in her arms. She glanced up at Matt and bit her lip over an impish smile. She'd notice.

Damn. He flicked the pager off with his thumbnail. This call might be the culmination of everything he'd worked to put together to lighten his professional burden. If he didn't take it he might be jeopardizing the future stability of his marriage. On the other hand, if he did take it he might well be jeopardizing the present tranquillity in his marriage.

Kyle let out another screech, screwing his beet red face up in the very personification of rage.

"This may take a while," Dani said to both Matt and Mr. Mussman.

"Maybe if you took him into the bathroom and wiped his face off with a cool rag," Matt suggested.

"Good idea." She nodded to Mr. Mussman to excuse herself.

Yes! Matt couldn't believe his luck. The instant she had left the room, he turned to the photographer and asked to use the phone.

"No, no, that's not good enough. I need a solid commitment right away. Tonight if possible." Matt tapped the toe of his wing tip on the hardwood floor of Mussman's cluttered office. "First thing tomorrow?" Matt groaned silently at the ceiling. "Well, I guess it will have to do, won't it?"

He gripped the phone until the beige plastic burned his dry palm. "Yeah, I understand. See you in the morning—first thing. Goodbye, Wayne."

Matt hung up and shot out of Mussman's office, thundering straight for the curtained room where Dani and Kyle would be waiting. When he pushed into the small cubicle, he found only Mussman, packing up his equipment.

"Where's my wife?" he asked, trying to make it sound casual.

"Gone." Mussman stuffed his camera into a big, padded bag.

"Gone? Where? When?"

As if to answer his question, the bell hanging above Mussman's studio door clanged followed by the definitive *wham* of the door slamming shut.

"Excuse me, Mr. Mussman," Matt called over his shoulder. The warped wood of the musty studio's floor creaked under his weight as he dashed after his wife. Outside, the warmth of the summer night swathed his face. He glanced up and down the street for Dani and might have missed her, if Kyle hadn't let out a cranky protest.

"Dani, wait." He rushed after her.

The heels of her good pumps pounded on the sidewalk, the rhythm accelerating.

"Dani, please, don't go off half-cocked. I have a very good reason for taking that phone call."

Her footsteps ceased. The light of a nearby streetlight cast a silvery aura over her head and shoulders and outlined Kyle's small body curled close to her. Dani's face remained obscured. Even so, Matt knew she had turned toward him. His own pace slackened, then stilled when he came close enough to sense the intensity of her rage.

"Look, honey," he said in a placating tone. "I just had to answer my page. I was expecting a very important call."

"An important call." Her voice sounded deceptively calm. "An important call? What about your family? What about Kyle and me? Aren't we important?"

"You know you are." He edged closer.

"How, Matt? How would I know that we're important to you?" Her voice remained strong but when she drew a breath, a tremble betrayed her pain. "You certainly don't put us before anything else, not even for a few minutes. It's just like the night you meant to propose to me."

"How?" He crossed his arms over his chest, assuming the lamplight allowed her to see the defensive pose. "Just how is this anything like that night in the restaurant?"

She groaned through clenched teeth. Even with her face obscured, he knew she had rolled her eyes. "Matt, this is exactly like that night. Then, like now, you had the chance— no, you made the opportunity—to put me first if even for one evening."

"And?"

"And you couldn't do it." She slapped her hand against her thigh. Kyle roused, then laid his head on her shoulder again. She continued in a hurried, hushed tone. "Forget about the promises you made about our future, you couldn't even put me first for an hour."

"Dani, you don't understand how imperative I felt it was that I answer those calls."

"No, you don't understand, Matt. I don't care if that was the president of the United States appointing you to the Supreme Court, it could have waited fifteen or twenty minutes."

"Dani, I..."

"Just fifteen or twenty minutes, Matt." Her voice cracked. "Just long enough to let me feel special, to let me pretend I'm the center of your world if only for a few moments."

"You are the center of my world, Dani," he whispered in voice so dry he feared the wind would blow it away like ust before Dani heard it.

"No, Matt." Light bounced off her thick curls as she hook her head. "I wanted to believe that could be true. I lmost deluded myself into thinking maybe..." A jagged igh tore away the end of her statement, then she tilted her ead up. "The evidence is in, counselor. The verdict is clear. know where I stand with you and it's only fair that you now where you stand with me."

"Dani, don't." He tried to swallow. He reached out for er but she slipped her arm away from his seeking finger- ips.

"Whatever my feelings for you may be, Matt, I can't live ike this. I only ask that if we're awarded Kyle, you stay with ne long enough to see the adoption through."

"I told you I'd do whatever you wanted, Dani," he heard imself saying.

"Fine. That's what I want." She turned. "Do you want o sleep in the master bedroom tonight or shall I?"

"You can." Without Dani, Matt doubted if he'd ever leep in that damn bed again. "I'll sleep in the guest room." Ie dug into his pocket and pulled out his car keys. They ingled in the silence. He choked back the bile rising in his hroat. "Here, you drive the baby home. It's so close, I'd ike to walk."

"Thank you," she whispered, taking the keys. She spun round and took a step. Her foot faltered. Matt rushed for- vard. She straightened, secured the baby, then brushed his and away. Head high, she strode away.

As she disappeared into the dark night, Matt mouthed his goodbyes. Goodbye to all his hopes and dreams. He ground is teeth together. Goodbye to all that really mattered in his ife. Every beat of his heart sent shards of pain through his ody.

Goodbye to the only woman he would ever love.

Chapter Twelve

It wasn't the alarm clock or her husband's gentle nudging that woke Dani bright and early. It was the sense of impending doom. The feeling overtook her so completely as she slept that it jolted her awake. She sat straight up—and immediately regretted it. Her stomach lurched, then settled to a queasy roll. She reached over Matt's undisturbed side of the bed and switched off the clock radio. A pang of remembered emotion plucked at her taut nerves.

Last night she had realized just how hopeless her marriage to Matt would be. Oh, they might have made it work for a year, maybe two. But soon, always coming in second to anyone who walked in the door of Matt Taylor, Attorney at Law, would wear away at her. Before long she would come to resent Matt just as she already resented the inordinate amount of time he lavished on his career. Then what would they have? Joint custody. Community property. Nothing.

She sighed and put her head in her hands. Somehow, she had to find the strength to keep the crippling heartache from showing today. Her chance to keep Kyle might very well depend on it.

Kyle. She fell back against her plump feather pillows and listened to see if the baby had awakened. In the distant downstairs, she could hear the sounds of Matt in the kitchen trying to coax the baby into eating some cereal. Might as well get up while they're both occupied, she decided glumly, because she really needed a few minutes of privacy.

Flinging the covers back, Dani leapt from the bed. An action that she quickly came to rue. In her mind, the floor did a brief imitation of a roller coaster. She grabbed the bedpost for support. After a moment, the world calmed and she was able to collect the package she'd picked up at the drugstore the night before. She stared down at the bright red box in her hand. As if she didn't have enough problems . . .

No, she told herself. She would not dwell on the negative or worry about a situation she wasn't even sure would materialize. Lifting her head, she marched into the master bathroom.

"Dani, honey, your mother's here to look after Kyle," Matt called a minute after she had safely cloistered herself in the bathroom.

She tore her gaze from the plastic tube in her hand and blinked at the closed door. No time to lose, she thought.

"Okay," she called out, picking up the test kit and reading frantically.

"What should I tell her?"

She squinted at the fine print. "Place upright and do not disturb."

"What?"

Think fast. She ran to put her shoulder to the door. "Um, tell Mom I'm uptight and not to disturb me."

"Are you all right, Dani?" He wriggled the doorknob.

Dani flattened her cheek to the cool wooden door. "Never mind . . . just tell her I'll be out in a minute," she said instead. More like fifteen, if she read the instructions right, she thought. "Okay?"

"Sure. I'm leaving now. I have something very important I want to discuss with Wayne Perry before the hearing. I'll see you at the courthouse in forty-five minutes."

"Matt?" She swung the door open but he had already left. She slumped her shoulders forward and sighed. It was probably for the best, she thought. No use getting him worked up until she knew for sure. As if she could know anything for sure with her whole life up in the air.

She sighed and cursed the tears that seemed to flow too easily these days. "Darn that man," she murmured. "If he would just give in a little. That's all I ask. Just a little."

But it was clearly asking too much. Just look at how anxious he was to get to the courthouse. Today, of all days, he should have lingered at least a little while to make sure she was all right. She swiped away the warm drops under her lashes.

What could she do about it now? Nothing, except go back to what she had been doing, then prepare herself for her day in court.

Matt thrummed his fingers on the stack of files sitting on the table before him. Where was Dani? The session was about to begin and he had so much he wanted to tell her. He scored his hand back through his hair while swinging his gaze around the room. The Delaney sisters sat beside Wayne Perry, their expressions serene. However this hearing went, Matt realized, they were prepared to handle it.

He wished he could say the same. With the big blowup last night, he and Dani hadn't spent any time discussing what would happen after the hearing today. He chuckled in bitter irony that everything he'd accomplished these past few

days to lessen his work load had come undone by his own
hands.

He sighed a curse through puffed-out cheeks, then
wrenched his wrist to expose his watch. A hand came down
to cover the white gold dial.

"I'm here," Dani said. She eased into the chair beside
him, her face pale.

"Where've you been?"

"All rise," the bailiff bellowed.

Dani smiled meekly at him and shrugged. They stood
amid the clamor of a dozen people getting to their feet. In a
matter of minutes, the proceedings were under way like a
mad horse race running headlong toward the finish line.

Wayne called that slug, Roger Grant, who cast a very grim
view of Dani. First he described her as a woman who had no
qualms about marrying without love. Then he launched into
a rehashing of their conversation outside the grocery store.
When he was done, the Delaneys both wore very satisfied
smiles. And they deserved them, too.

"Psst." Dani tugged at Matt's sleeve. "Put me on the
stand."

Her demeanor had changed. Fierce determination that
had not been there earlier shone in her pretty face. She was
up to something and it was his job to make sure that
"something" didn't land her in jail. He flicked her hand
away and shook his head. "No. I will not put you on the
stand."

"But you have to," she whispered.

He bent his head to put his mouth to her ear. "I don't
have to and I won't."

"Why not?" She slapped her open hand on the table. "I
have to go up there and refute what he said."

"Exactly." He gripped his pen in his hand. "And the only
way you can refute what he said is to lie. I may not be able

to win this case, but I refuse to let you go up there and per-jure yourself." He sat up straight, cutting her off.

"Matt." She yanked his sleeve again.

"No." He kept his eyes forward.

She glared at him so hard he could feel the heat of it on his profile, but he held his position.

"All right then," she snapped. Suddenly she leaned forward, her face low to the table. *"Psst."*

Matt turned to find her pointing to herself and then to the stand. He followed her line of vision and saw Wayne Perry grinning and nodding.

"Dani, no..."

"Your Honor, I'd like to call as my next witness, Danielle Taylor."

Matt shot his hand out to capture her wrist but she slid away too quickly. His fingers balled into a fist over the empty place where her hand had rested. He hung his head.

After swearing her in and a few preliminary questions, Wayne focused his attention on the questions Matt dreaded hearing. "Mrs. Taylor, do you recall the conversation Mr. Grant recounted just a few minutes ago?"

"Yes, I do."

Matt watched warily, ready to spring up with an objection should Wayne push too far or Dani start to perjure herself.

"Do you deny making any of the statements he quoted you as saying on that day?"

"No, I don't deny any of the statements."

Wayne pivoted, a broad smile on his face. Matt glared at him and he immediately sobered.

"I made those statements," Dani continued. "But not the way he said I made them."

Matt shifted forward in his seat, the balls of his feet pressed against the floor.

"Oh?" Wayne looked at her over his shoulder.

Dani wet her lips. Even under these circumstances, Matt thought she was the most beautiful woman he'd ever known. She tossed back her dark curls and tipped her chin up.

"Roger said I was flirtatious. Which is pretty silly when just two seconds earlier he told everyone that I never even pretended to be in love with him."

Matt chuckled.

"All right, Mrs. Taylor, we'll concede that you weren't flirting with Mr. Grant." Wayne opened his mouth to ask another question but Dani preempted him.

"I was mad," she said.

"I beg your pardon?" Wayne shook back his blond hair.

"My husband and I had just cut our honeymoon short to come back and deal with all the vicious rumors Roger had been spreading. When I saw him that day I was practically looking for a fight."

That was probably the truth, Matt decided.

"I shouldn't have said those things, I know." She looked up a bit too adoringly at Judge Harcourt. "But all I could think of was getting Roger to stop spreading lies about my marriage."

"Objection, Your Honor," Wayne bellowed. "There's been no evidence that anything Mr. Grant has said about the Taylors' marriage is a falsehood."

"Falsehood?" Dani yelped. "They were barefaced lies, Your Honor. He said we didn't have a 'real marriage,' that there was no commitment between us, he implied that we weren't..." She cast her eyes down. "Intimate."

"All quite disturbing, Mrs. Taylor, but Mr. Grant does have a right to express his opinion as long as it's not slanderous. And since there's no real way to prove his statements are false I'll have to sustain Mr. Perry's objection." He lifted his gavel.

"But I have proof," Dani said quietly to the floor.

"What did you say?" Judge Harcourt's gavel wavered.

Matt watched in awe as Dani threw her slender shoulders back and told the judge, "I have proof that Matthew Taylor and I have had the kind of marriage Roger calls 'real.'"

"I object," Matt announced, bolting up from his chair.

"To what?" Judge Harcourt scowled at him.

He studied Dani's face from the blush on her cheeks to the determined tilt of her chin. He plunked himself back down in his seat. "I withdraw my objection."

"Well, I haven't withdrawn mine," Wayne reminded everyone a bit too loudly.

"Sit down, Mr. Perry," the judge barked. "Now, Mrs. Taylor, if you can offer some real proof that Mr. Grant spread unfounded gossip about you, I'd like to hear it."

"Your Honor," Wayne interjected from his seat. "Mr. Grant is not on trial here."

"I'm aware of that, thank you, Mr. Perry." The judge's expression warned the other lawyer. But when he turned to Dani, his features seemed to melt. "Now, Danielle, what proof do you have that you and Matthew have a—" he sputtered a soft cough through his fist "—valid marriage?"

Dani dropped her gaze to her lap.

Matt tensed. If she could pull this off, the Delaneys' star witness would be discredited. But if she lied to do it, he'd have to intercede before she got herself in big trouble. He inched to the edge of his seat.

"Well?" the judge prodded.

She sank her white teeth into her red lip and her green-eyed gaze into Matt's.

He pressed his fingertips to the tabletop, ready to leap up and stop her.

"The proof I have that this is a valid marriage, in every intimate way is . . ."

Matt grit his teeth.

"I'm pregnant."

The tiny courtroom crowd burst into pandemonium. Matt bounded to his feet, his voice full volume, "Your Honor, I..."

"You what, son?"

Matt's gaze fixed on Dani's. His mouth hung open as her words sank in. He tilted his head. She nodded the silent answer to his need for verification.

"I want permission to hug the witness," he said.

"Permission granted." The gavel came down with a resounding thud again.

Matt rushed to the witness stand and took Dani in his arms. "This is great news."

"Is it? I was afraid it would be overwhelming, with the strain on our marriage because of..."

"Because of my working too much," he finished. He grinned and pulled her closer. "Well, I have a little earth-shaking news on that front." He put his mouth to her ear to whisper, "You know that big project I've been devoting so much time to?"

She nodded her head warily.

"Well, I can finally tell you what that was about." He bent his head to peer into her eyes. "About an hour ago, Wayne Perry agreed to form a partnership with me. He's cutting Roger Grant loose as a client and is hot to take on a big chunk of my casework."

She drew back. "But why would you...?"

"To make more time for you and my family. If you still want that."

"Oh, yes. Yes." She threw her arms around him again. "I love you, Matt."

"I love you, too, Dani, more than I can ever express."

Tears of joy washed over her cheeks. Never in her wildest dreams could she have imagined better news. After all the years of waiting, she had everything she ever wanted—and then some.

Matt showered her face with tiny kisses. Finally his mouth covered hers. She responded with all the love she finally felt free to share. He curled her tightly to his chest and she lost herself in him. Until the incessant pounding of a gavel and the call for order brought them back to the present.

When the courtroom quieted, Judge Harcourt beamed down at them like some smug little cherub. "So, in light of this news, do you two still want to pursue custody of the Delaney child?"

Dani looked up at her wonderful husband. He grinned back at her. "Absolutely, sir. Now, more than ever, we understand the wishes of our friends, Karen and Bill Delaney, in wanting their child to be cared for in a loving home."

Matt glanced up. "Not that the Delaney sisters aren't loving people. But in our home we can offer a brother or sister."

"Or both, given enough time," Dani added. Matt wrapped his arm around her and kissed her temple.

"The point is, Your Honor, that we have more than enough love to go around."

Judge Harcourt's sappy smile hardened as he turned to address Wayne and his clients, Sarah and Veronica Delaney. "Do you have anything more to add to the proceedings?"

Veronica leaned over to Wayne. Wisps of blond hair moved gently as she spoke into his ear. When he straightened away, a huge grin adorned his face. "Your Honor, my clients wish to withdraw their petition for custody of the minor child, Kyle Matthew Delaney, with the provision that the Taylors agree to a reasonable visitation arrangement with the Delaney family."

Judge Harcourt swung his gaze to Matt and Dani.

"We have no problem with that, Your Honor," Matt said.

"Then it's done." The gavel came down for the final time.

Two hours later, with Kyle tucked safely and happily in his very own crib, Dani and Matt curled up on their bed.

"Well, I guess we'll have to save the champagne we were going to use to toast Kyle's adoption for after the baby's born." Matt smoothed his hand down her abdomen.

She laid her head back on his shoulder and let the thrill of his nearness engross her. He was the handsomest, the smartest, the sexiest man alive. And he was hers. She snuggled closer, laying her hand over his heart on his naked chest. "You don't mind too much, do you Matt, that we went straight from wedding bells to diaper pins?"

He laughed. With one finger he tipped her face up. "Well, I wouldn't have minded having a little more of a honeymoon."

She smiled dreamily. "Maybe we can sneak away to Rosemont House for a long weekend before the baby arrives. Mom would be happy to baby-sit Kyle."

"Maybe." He kissed her nose. "We'll just start our honeymoon right now."

His lips found hers and she surrendered to the delicious sensation and to her husband's delightful suggestion.

COMING NEXT MONTH

**#1096 THE WOMEN IN JOE SULLIVAN'S LIFE—
Marie Ferrarella**

Fabulous Fathers

Bachelor Joe Sullivan thought he had enough women in his life
when his three nieces came to live with him. But once he met
Maggie McGuire, he knew this pretty woman would make his family
complete.

#1097 BABY TALK—Julianna Morris

Bundles of Joy

Cassie Cavannaugh was ready to have a baby—and she'd found
the perfect father in sexy Jake O'Connor. Too bad Jake wanted
nothing to do with kids—and everything to do with Cassie!

#1098 COWBOY FOR HIRE—Dorsey Kelley

Wranglers and Lace

Cowboy Bent Murray didn't need anyone—especially not a sassy
young thing like Kate Monahan. And no matter how good Kate
felt in his arms, he would never let her into his heart....

#1099 IMITATION BRIDE—Christine Scott

When handsome Michael Damian asked Lacey Keegan to be
his pretend bride, Lacey could only say yes. Now she hoped her
make-believe groom would become her real-life husband.

#1100 SECOND CHANCE AT MARRIAGE—Pamela Dalton

The last thing Dina Paxton and Gabriel Randolph wanted was
marriage. But sharing a home made them feel very much like man
and wife. Now if they could just keep from falling in love....

#1101 AN IMPROBABLE WIFE—Sally Carleen

Straitlaced Carson Thayer didn't even *like* his new tenant, so
how could he be falling for her? What was it about Emily James
that made him want to do crazy things—like get married!

MILLION DOLLAR SWEEPSTAKES (III)

No purchase necessary. To enter, follow the directions published. Method of entry may vary. For eligibility, entries must be received no later than March 31, 1996. No liability is assumed for printing errors, lost, late or misdirected entries. Odds of winning are determined by the number of eligible entries distributed and received. Prizewinners will be determined no later than June 30, 1996.

Sweepstakes open to residents of the U.S. (except Puerto Rico), Canada, Europe and Taiwan who are 18 years of age or older. All applicable laws and regulations apply. Sweepstakes offer void wherever prohibited by law. Values of all prizes are in U.S. currency. This sweepstakes is presented by Torstar Corp., its subsidiaries and affiliates, in conjunction with book, merchandise and/or product offerings. For a copy of the Official Rules send a self-addressed, stamped envelope (WA residents need not affix return postage) to: MILLION DOLLAR SWEEPSTAKES (III) Rules, P.O. Box 4573, Blair, NE 68009, USA.

EXTRA BONUS PRIZE DRAWING

No purchase necessary. The Extra Bonus Prize will be awarded in a random drawing to be conducted no later than 5/30/96 from among all entries received. To qualify, entries must be received by 3/31/96 and comply with published directions. Drawing open to residents of the U.S. (except Puerto Rico), Canada, Europe and Taiwan who are 18 years of age or older. All applicable laws and regulations apply; offer void wherever prohibited by law. Odds of winning are dependent upon number of eligibile entries received. Prize is valued in U.S. currency. The offer is presented by Torstar Corp., its subsidiaries and affiliates in conjunction with book, merchandise and/or product offering. For a copy of the Official Rules governing this sweepstakes, send a self-addressed, stamped envelope (WA residents need not affix return postage) to: Extra Bonus Prize Drawing Rules, P.O. Box 4590, Blair, NE 68009, USA.

SWP-S795

He's Too Hot To Handle...but she can take a little heat.

As a *Privileged Woman,*
you'll be entitled to all
these *Free Benefits.*
And *Free Gifts,* too.

To thank you for buying our books, we've designed an exclusive FREE program called *PAGES & PRIVILEGES*™. You can enroll with just one Proof of Purchase, and get the kind of luxuries that, until now, you could only read about.

BIG HOTEL DISCOUNTS

A privileged woman stays in the finest hotels. And so can you—at up to 60% off! Imagine standing in a hotel check-in line and watching as the guest in front of you pays $150 for the same room that's only costing you $60. Your *Pages & Privileges* discounts are good at Sheraton, Marriott, Best Western, Hyatt and thousands of other fine hotels all over the U.S., Canada and Europe.

FREE DISCOUNT TRAVEL SERVICE

A privileged woman is always jetting to romantic places. When <u>you</u> fly, just make one phone call for the lowest published airfare at time of booking—<u>or double the difference back!</u> PLUS— you'll get a $25 voucher to use the first time you book a flight AND <u>5% cash back on every ticket you buy thereafter through the travel service!</u>

*F*REE GIFTS!

A privileged woman is always getting wonderful gifts.
Luxuriate in rich fragrances that will stir your senses (and his). This gift-boxed assortment of fine perfumes includes three popular scents, each in a beautiful designer bottle. <u>Truly Lace</u>...This luxurious fragrance unveils your sensuous side. <u>L'Effleur</u>...discover the romance of the Victorian era with this soft floral. <u>Muguet des bois</u>...a single note floral of singular beauty.

YOURS FREE!

$50 VALUE

*F*REE INSIDER TIPS LETTER

A privileged woman is always informed. And you'll be, too, with our free letter full of fascinating information and sneak previews of upcoming books.

*M*ORE GREAT GIFTS & BENEFITS TO COME

A privileged woman always has a lot to look forward to. And so will you. You get all these wonderful FREE gifts and benefits now with only one purchase...and there are no additional purchases required. However, each additional retail purchase of Harlequin and Silhouette books brings you a step closer to even more great FREE benefits like half-price movie tickets... and even more FREE gifts.

L'Effleur...This basketful of romance lets you discover L'Effleur from head to toe, heart to home.

Truly Lace...
A basket spun with the sensuous luxuries of Truly Lace, including Dusting Powder in a reusable satin and lace covered box.

Complete the Enrollment Form in the front of this book and mail it with this Proof of Purchase.

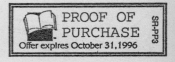

PROOF OF PURCHASE
Offer expires October 31, 1996

SR-PP3